FIRST HORSES

WESTERN LITERATURE SERIES

Western Trails: A Collection of Short Stories by Mary Austin
selected and edited by Melody Graulich

Cactus Thorn by Mary Austin
with foreword and afterword by Melody Graulich

Dan De Quille, the Washoe Giant
A Biography and Anthology
prepared by Richard A. Dwyer and Richard E. Lingenfelter

Desert Wood: An Anthology of Nevada Poets
edited by Shaun T. Griffin

The City of Trembling Leaves
by Walter Van Tilburg Clark

Many Californias: Literature from the Golden State
edited by Gerald W. Haslam

The Authentic Death of Hendry Jones
by Charles Neider

First Horses: Stories of the New West
by Robert Franklin Gish

UNIVERSITY OF NEVADA PRESS
RENO   LAS VEGAS   LONDON

FIRST
HORSES

STORIES OF THE NEW WEST

ROBERT FRANKLIN GISH

Foreword by Gordon A. Weaver

Western Literature Series Editor: John H. Irsfeld

The paper used in this book meets the requirements of American National
Standard for Information Sciences—Permanence of Paper for Printed Library
Materials, ANSI Z39.48-1984. Binding materials were selected for
strength and durability.

Library of Congress Cataloging-in-Publication Data

Gish, Robert.
First horses : stories of the new West / Robert Franklin Gish ;
foreword by Gordon A. Weaver.
p.   cm. — (Western literature series)
ISBN 0-87417-210-1 (cloth)
ISBN 0-87417-211-x (pbk.)
1. Western stories.   2. West (U.S.)—Fiction.   I. Title.
II. Series.
PS3557.I79F55   1993
813'.54—dc20   92-31540
                                                                   CIP

University of Nevada Press, Reno, Nevada 89557 USA
Copyright © 1993 by University of Nevada Press
All rights reserved
Book design by Susan Gutnik
Printed in the United States of America

2   4   6   8   9   7   5   3

To Judy, Robin, Tim, and Annabeth.
To Lillian and the memory of Jess.
To the new Butzier boys, Matthew and Joseph.
And to Eddie and Teri and the South Valley.

And those poor creatures were thereupon so stigmatized . . .
that they will bear the marks of them to their dying day!
—Cotton Mather, *Magnalia Christi Americana*

CONTENTS

FOREWORD

MOST SHORT STORY COLLECTIONS FALL INTO ONE OF THREE BASIC types. Least common is the short story cycle, a gathering of tales that on occasion reads like a loosely constructed novel; Sherwood Anderson's *Winesburg, Ohio* and James Joyce's *Dubliners* are classic examples, and Mark Costello's *Murphy Stories* is a more contemporary collection. In these works the reader usually finds a common locale, a character or characters reappearing from story to story, and a narrative that unifies the assembled fictions. A second type brings together stories that, however varied the subjects, all dramatize a common theme. The Hispanic-American voices in the recently celebrated work of Sandra Cisneros illustrate one basis for grouping stories to make a volume. The focus of her interest lies in an all but polemic protest at the cultural and racial oppression that one minority group experienced at the hands of an indifferent or malevolent society. Raymond Carver's blue-collar and alcoholic lowlifes, dwelling in trailer courts, isolated and immobile, are in much the same situation. Finally, authors can offer story collections designed to showcase their virtuosity by providing a wide range of subjects, structures, and styles that will dazzle a reader into recognizing the authors' talent and craft. The late—and great—John O'Hara exulted more than once, in print, at the scope of his prowess in this regard.

What is both interesting and impressive about Robert Gish's *First Horses: Stories of the New West* is that this debut collection of stories exhibits something of all of the above as its *raison d'etre*. *First Horses* embodies what seems almost a systematic survey of a geographical region and its culture, with rich variations of character and narrative that delineate the subjects. The theme that animates Gish's fiction is highlighted by his epigraph from Cotton Mather, a seminal and ambiguous Puritan father dedicated to what has become the distinctly American need to locate and examine the moral meaning of our history. In secularizing the quote from Mather, the stories in *First Horses* exemplify the contention that one's region, one's culture, one's ancestral history stamp a man's or woman's character with the definitive terms of both identity and destiny. If Cotton Mather is talking about sin and, by implication, moral heritage, Gish cites him to tell the reader that his stories bear witness to the proposition that we are all like his characters—creatures formed as much by our forebears and our peers as by our conscious will or our unconscious motives.

First Horses also serves as a broad panorama for Robert Gish to ply the reader with his capacity for a sweep of characters and events that strikes one as nearly limitless. Gish's sensibility is not restricted to men or women, the young or middle aged or old; neither is it confined to one or another social stratum, focused exclusively on a high or middle or lowbrow milieu. *First Horses* offers a fictional horn of plenty, inviting the reader to experience a most generous potpourri of humanity's ambitions and failures in a language and style suited to create the maximum effect.

In "Blessed" we listen to the tortured voice of Coreen, gifted with the power to heal with the touch of her hands and her breath. This "blessing" is a curse to her, a heritage she has endured since childhood, and we share the twisted argument she conducts with herself as she struggles to accept who and what she is, what she must be if she is to be herself. In the intimacy of her most interior consciousness, in the texture of her innermost voice, we hear the echoes of our Puritan founders, of Cotton Mather, blessed and cursed by his Calvinist God, denied a clear vision of His visage, as Coreen was denied her father.

In this collection's title story, we see the author's ability to sustain a context that is, in and of itself, of minimal apparent consequence. On the surface, the Bronco Cafe is no stage suited to high drama but is rendered by Robert Gish to be a kind of microcosm in which a complex of emotions and primitive impulses plays out its course. Taking a distanced stance, the narrator introduces us to Florinda, Lucy, Abrán, Reuben, and the exotic Buddy Tedrick, and we watch them dance about the topic of a bowl of chili while the conflict of Hispanic, Native American, and Anglo cultures hovers over them like a miasma. If the conclusion suggests a happy resolution, it is a tenuous one at best.

The narrator of "Fiesta" is a college boy, a musician, a would-be sophisticate who tells his story with only a partial sense of the guilt that drives his utterance. The debacle of the fight that costs a friend his eye results, the story reveals to the reader but not the narrator, from a pathetic attempt to assume an identity that is as fraudulent as the "fiesta" presented on a campus for the amusement of the student body. Trying to be what you are not, "Fiesta" tells us, is not only absurd, it is dangerous.

In "Salvation" the legacy of Mather is readily recognized. Pastor Ron's evangelical fundamentalism is both his strength and his weakness. His seduction of Lavola, the church pianist—or was he the seduced?—is couched in the same intensity and profundity as his Protestant faith, and the guilt this transgression triggers lives as deeply within him as his Baptist upbringing. Full-immersion baptism will not wash away the sin of Pastor Ron and his Lavola. Pastor Ron's successful prayer for the recovery of Lavola's stricken son is, ironically, the means by which her husband Thestal discovers their adultery. A final irony resides in Thestal's hymn, sung over the body of Pastor Ron, whom he has just murdered.

Gustav, the narrator of "Neonate," ruminates on the life and death (by suicide) of a surrogate father, Doc. The story is ostensibly an elegy for Doc, but the true subject is the narrator's futile attempt to articulate the meaning of Doc's life. Gustav is a "neon artist," and his story parallels the artist's need to isolate and reveal the significance of human experience. Doc, who kills himself when he is exposed as an abortionist, represents a type of human nature: competence and even decency that is flawed by moral failure. The story's narrator, try as he does, cannot translate the meaning of experience into viable terms of moral awareness and behavior. Gustav's final vision in the story is of Las Vegas, a city of glitter and illusion, a monument to the fatal distinctions between surface appearance and its dark moral underside. It is not coincidental that most of the story's narrative has to do with fishing for sharks, symbols of the grim and bloody dimension of humanity.

And this is but a sampling of the generous fare in Robert Gish's *First Horses: Stories of the New West*. It is a collection rich in variety, crafted in execution, and unified by its ambitious confrontation with universal concerns. It is a remarkable debut in the short fiction genre and will delight and reward its readers.

GORDON A. WEAVER
Oklahoma State University

PREFACE

I WROTE THESE STORIES IN TRIBUTE, MOST ESPECIALLY, TO THAT area where I grew up in Albuquerque, New Mexico, known as the South Valley, and to some of the people I knew there in my youth. It was my corner of the American West at mid-century and my family and friends were, for me, representative of that particular era's version of the Westerner. Like the American West itself, Albuquerque is not a monolithic place. The Heights and the Valley and the Foothills divide again and again into Downtown, University, Nob Hill, West Mesa, North Valley, Corrales, Bosque Farms, Martinez Town, Five Points, Atrisco, Barelas, San Jose, Los Padillas, and many other areas and neighborhoods. Each of these regions proves how diverse and complex the culture, class structure, and ambiance of a modern Western metropolis can be and indicates how varied the larger West itself is—in its societies, its geography, its history, and its story.

More and more we are coming to realize that the Rocky Mountain West is not the Pacific West or the Southwest anymore than the Native American West is the Hispanic West or the Anglo-American West or any other of the ethnic Wests we see around us. Throughout the years and especially at present we have learned to see clearly how women in the West have influenced the region and are influenced by it in ways that are quite different from those of men. Even the concept of the West, although clearly convenient for certain historical and cultural orientations, is seemingly more and more ethnocentric in its origins and demarcations.

Although the various lives and landscapes replicated in these stories are now part of my own, the region's, and the century's past, they remain *new* in my imagination. It is a phenomenon that is not merely a process but the substance of the *West*. It is hoped that these stories will revive memories of the West for readers of my generation and create images in younger readers' minds of the then *new*, yet transitional, West of the 1950s—a once relatively naive but now paradoxically nostalgic place that was reawakened quite pleasurably for me in the writing of these narratives.

As we approach the end of this century, long after the alleged closing of the American frontier, we remember anew that the West is regenerative in each person's development and individuation and invites continuous revision in our appraisal of its significance. The once-predominant Anglo-European western *story* of discovery, exploration, and settlement—is now only one plot in countless plots of stories being told and heard; thus allowing the heretofore disenfranchised, so-called "minority voices," a fuller say as the balances and designations of minority/majority shift into new political and demographic configurations.

Regardless of our individual or family heritage, western history and story are anything but unidimensional and are every bit as much made up of persons of darker skin as by white, by women as by men. The exoticism of the western story is now more relative, more transvaluated than the many past masters of western fiction could ever have imagined; but the many new western writers know this well and demonstrate it in their work.

The Native American presence, and the Chicano presence in particular, remain strong influences in my life. In these stories I try to portray the recognition that the Southwest I first knew, the West which was my birthplace, was multicultural in its mixes and laminations much beyond anything described by the terminology of present-day "political correctness." Although African Americans and Asian Americans were less prominent in my early experiences (as they are in these stories), for me they exist in life and literature much beyond caricature and stereotype. My encounters with all of these peoples have formed and solidified my view of the present West in California, where western lands and the lives upon them still determine me and the subjects for my writing.

Now at the century's end, more than ever, the relativity of "westness" and of "otherness" make the American West both our collective past and our future as a nation. *First Horses: Stories of the New West* seeks to portray and dramatize this invigorating realization. These stories of the new West are, however, intended not to instruct but to entertain. For it is the West at its best, its most celebratory and sanguine, that wills us all to the next new day, the next new and youthful West, and the stories on the horizon waiting to be imagined, written, and read.

BLESSED

"Behold, I set before you this day a blessing and a curse."
—Deuteronomy 11:26

I REMEMBER MY HIDING PLACE. EVEN NOW I CAN FEEL THE COLD linoleum floor. See the small red flowers against the gray, slick surface. See the dust and lint on my legs and my socks. See the round metal legs and their little wheels, and sense the black, intricate bedsprings as I traced them, again and again, with my fingers, slipping off now and again into the soft white-and-gray-striped mattress. There were stains of various colors of yellow and brown that I could see through the springs—stains I always tried to avoid as I pushed my hand along the wires. I played a game with myself as I waited, more than one game, really. But the one I remember playing the most was trying not to touch one of those splotches of fading colors, some of which spread into other stains, touching, or almost touching. They were like little continents, small-shaped emblems of human history, family history really. My mother's history. My history. I hadn't caused any of the darker stains. When my mother turned the mattress, bemoaning the accidents occasioned there, she told me such things came with growing up, with becoming a woman. It was her bed, her room, where she slept alone in the fine, clean sheets. Under the beautiful patchwork quilt that she and my grandmother had made. Somehow I imagined that the bright and patterned swatches of old dresses, clothes, and remnants of material in the quilt had soaked through the bed covers and sheets, through the pads and the mattress itself to the underside. Where I would hide when people came. Came like the stains seeping through the mattress, to change the cheerful, controlled color and beauty of the quilt into the faded, random stains. I wondered if my father had slept on that bed with my mother. Had been healthy there on it, tall and warm and loving. I know he had been ill for some time. My mother told me about that time. I would ask her. And she would tell me about it, about how it all came to be and how I came to be this way. I would try to compare her different versions of how he got sick and what happened. How it affected her in her condition. I know that my mother cared for him in the room. Their room. This bed. And I know that he died in it. And after he died, only twenty-one days later, my mother told me I was born in the same bed and the same room where my father had died. I was born without ever seeing him. In person. Born where he died. And that's how they said I came to be blessed. That's why I always ran back to my mother's and once upon a time my father's room. To the one room in the old house that was part of all of us. Where I had started. And there I would try to trace back, try to think through how being blessed could be a curse—like the topside and bottom side of the bed. Like the darker bloodstains I tried to avoid touching when I waited, hiding, for the door to open and for my mother or my little sister to come after me and say they were here. The sick people were here, waiting for me. And I must come.

I remember when it started. And I remember when it ended. When I grew big enough and strong enough to resist, refusing to hide under the bed anymore. That last time I simply opened the bedroom door, picked up the paperweight, the glass-enclosed photo of my father, and sat down on the bed. Sat down on top of the quilt, with my feet finally touching the floor. And when Rosie came for me, by now herself tired of our ritual, I just said, "Not this time. Not ever again." And I walked out into the front room and told them that I was sorry but that I couldn't share my blessing, couldn't bless their little boy, couldn't touch him and blow on him and heal him. And they all knew that I meant it. I remember too the expressions on their faces and what I still believe was relief in my mother's eyes that our blessing and our burden had passed. We wouldn't talk about it again. Not until many years later, when my mother came to live with us, after I had married and moved away and had you and your brothers. And then, as she was sewing or sitting in her chair reading or helping with the meals, she would sometimes bring up how as a girl I was blessed. Always would be, she insisted.

And now, with you here tonight, so feverish, so ill, for the first time I will try to pray back my blessing, see if I can believe that I was blessed and in so believing bless you, my special daughter, so that you may recover and live into your own womanhood, and pass along your birthright, your own special blessing in the lives of those you will meet and merge with, your family in the larger family.

I see you in the concern and love of your father, a father who has held you. I see you in the worry of my mother, your grandmother, and her urging me to use my special gift of healing. I see you, too, in the reflection of my father, his heavy, mounded picture, now there on the dresser in this room where I rock with you and bathe your face and soft little body.

I remember the last time. And I remember the first time and all those times in between, building over those disappearing years of my childhood to this moment when I must remember and believe and hope that the believing won't ruin it. For I didn't really "believe" when I was asked to do it. Didn't really think about the results of what I was doing. I just remember the hot and flushed faces of the people I was taken to. Faces so different from the glass-encased, cool face of my father, his paperweight hair long and parted in the middle, flaring out over his forehead and his face. His black coat and high-collared white shirt. His tie looking fake, painted on in some false sense of touch-up rightness, the same kind of falseness, no doubt, arranged, later, on his coffined face, drained of life by the fever and the diphtheria. Had he lived and held me, breathed on me and kissed me, would I not have been truly blessed? Why in his dying and my never knowing him, except in this one photo, is there blessing? What logic, what convolution of superstitious belief reversed things so?

I can see my mother coming out of the house now, coming off the porch, calling for me. "Coreen, where are you, child? We have company. They want to see you." I had been at the side of the house, playing in the hollyhocks, watching the bees fly into the flowers, listening to them in their loudness. I wasn't very old, five or six. And I remember my mother picking me up and carrying me inside the house, stopping by the basin of water on the porch, to wash my face, and my hands, and to give me a drink of water. And I remember the boy, older than me, seated in the front room, in Lee's chair while Lee, my stepfather, talked to the boy's father and mother. "This little boy's sick, Coreen. He has a sore throat. And we want you to blow in it and make him feel better." My mother led me over to the boy, and he looked at me and at his mother and father. And then his eyes closed and his head drooped and I remember his father shaking his shoulder and telling him to open his mouth. And I remember Lee picking me up and putting my face close to the boy's and telling me, "Go ahead. Blow a big breath right into his mouth." And his breath was hot and bad-smelling, but I blew into it. And then Lee put me down on the floor, and without thinking I ran into my mother's bedroom. And I picked up the paperweight with my father's picture beneath the glass and I held it tight and waited until I watched the man and woman carry the boy out to their buggy and saw them head out over the hill toward the main road and the mailbox. And I was glad they were gone. But the boy's hot face and his breath stayed with me, around my face. And I put my father's glassed picture against my cheek and on my forehead and felt its coolness.

Then more people came. Sometimes at night. And I had to blow in their mouths, or on cuts and sores. Or I had to touch people's feet and legs and arms. I had to touch broken ankles. I had to blow into the ears of old people. And soon I ran to the bedroom before they found me. Ran when I saw anybody walk or ride over the hill. Ran from wagons when they came or, now and then, from cars as they kicked up dust as far away as the mailbox, turning off the main road, coming to me. Coming to be cured. What sorrow I felt for them was overcome by repulsion—and sorrow for myself that I had to be so humiliated, although at first I didn't isolate that particular emotion. It just wasn't pleasant. The people were sick. You could tell it in the touch—feverish or clammy. You could tell it by the odors, the smells of sickness lingering in their hair, their clothes. And so I would hide under the bed and gain whatever courage came from that room, that place. Knowing they knew where I always ran. Knowing that if I didn't come for Rosie, then my mother would come. And then if I still wouldn't crawl out from under the bed Lee would come and without saying anything reach back and pull me, grimacing and whining, across the gray and red floral linoleum.

And tonight, with you in my arms, rocking back and forth to my whispers and rememberings I must go back, beyond Doc Hall's prescriptions, beyond the prayers of Reverend Green, of family and friends, beyond the home remedies of your grandmother Fronie, beyond my ancient terrors and revulsions when I would hug myself, rock myself past the contours of quilt and mattress stain back to whatever thoughts my father might have had about me in his illness, in his health during the early months of my mother's pregnancy, or in his delirium just before he died. Back to the thoughts and love he must have had for his unborn, unseen child and his wish for me to be here tonight with you, blessed as I am, and now with my very life's and love's breath, offering to you whatever strength and power and life-willing I can against sickness, whatever stay against death, whatever blessing.

HAT CHECK

"THAT'S ME WITH THE HAT ON," HE WOULD SAY, AS HE WALKED
around the dining room passing out his campaign card. And only him
in the photo! Couples would interrupt conversations, families would
stop eating, single diners would suspend soup spoons midway to
their mouths, servers would stand back, calmly holding hot coffee-
pots—all trying to oblige him as he made the rounds at Polly's Cafeteria, or Anaya's Cafe, or an open house or rally.

"Hope to get your vote come election day," he would say. Or
"Democrat for county commissioner—Rudy Lovato. Sure hope to
see you at the polls." Or just "Rudy Lovato's the name. Appreciate
your vote." He had a hundred variations on the combined introduction and sales pitch. I had heard just about all of them and could read
not just his lips but his mind.

He would stand by the tables of those willing to respond to
him—maybe they would pause and wipe their mouths with a napkin
and extend a hand for a brisk, politician handshake. Sometimes,
from my vantage point by the cashier or outside on the sidewalk,
seeing him work the room inside, it would look like he was helping
choking customers cough up a lodged chicken bone with a forceful
few pats on the back.

He was a tall man—a Hispano—made taller by his hand-tooled
cowboy boots, and by the Western-cut pants and shirts he wore.
Without his hat, with his bald head gleaming in the reflections of
the ceiling lights, he looked even taller. And with his hat on, which

was most of the time, he had an imposing, almost a looming presence.

He was sincere in his campaign and his exchange with people. He truly did want to become county commissioner, and as an insurance underwriter, trying to build an agency, he had some practical motive to know about bonding and zoning projects and road projections and revenues—all the business of the Valencia County Commission.

And he did truly like people, enjoyed them. Especially the Anglos. His own people, the Spanish and Mexican population, the people of the barrios, he pretty much ignored. I was part of that, too, as an Anglo myself. He felt the Anglos, the gringos, had the power. He enjoyed himself, too, for he was one of the most selfish, self-centered, and yet one of the most insecure men I've ever known. I tried to tell him that he was wrong in spending so much time with Anglos, in trying to fit in with us, in neglecting his own people. Why couldn't he live in both cultures? But all his one-sided, Anglo ways cost him more than a minor political campaign.

His larger campaign, though, one that had been under way long before his campaign for a seat on the commission, was to have people like him, to have me like him. As he explained it to me, jokingly almost, he started balding quite young, and by the time he was twenty-six or so he was completely bald. It bothered him. Embarrassed him. Hit at his male pride.

He didn't try to hide his baldness or compensate for it by wearing what hair he still had unusually long. He kept his hair around his temples and over his ears and around his neck quite short. But there was the hat. Always the hat. He relied more than usual on his hat. Always wore it when he was outside, announcing at the neighborhood weekend rodeos. Always wore it when he was calling square dances for the Los Amigos Square Dance and Cloggers Club where he boasted of membership.

And in his photographs, whether for family, clubs, or political publicity, he posed, smiling, with his hat on. He wore wide-brimmed, only partially blocked Resistol hats—almost just like they came out of the box—in the fall and winter. But every May, on the first day of the month, he switched to a straw hat, still cowboy style, but white straw.

For him May 1 was a landmark day each year: Straw Hat Day. He just couldn't have enjoyed wearing a hat as much as he did—just for the sake of hats and hatness. He had to be relying on a hat as some kind of compensation for being bald. In the summer, his hat kept his head from sunburn, sure. In the fall and winter and early spring, his hat kept his head warm, sure. But there was something psychological going on too.

He had an unusual respect for his hats—regardless of the season. No one close to him ever fooled with his hats in any way. He brushed them and had the initials "RL" embossed on the leather bands. When he went into a restaurant like Polly's, he would carefully position his hat on the highest shelf in the coatroom, placing it out of harm's way, trying to guard against its being taken by mistake or mashed.

I didn't mind it so much at first. More than most people would have guessed, he needed that kind of support, that kind of convenience—that kind of security, even power, in the face of the glances we would inevitably get when we walked into a restaurant or a reception together.

When I first came out here, when we first met, he was already high on everything about the Anglo, middle-class life—their houses, their cars, their jobs. He thought of our dating as part of the natural assimilation of the American way, "Americanization," that kind of thing. And I agreed. But I wanted to know more about his people, his heritage, the Hispanic West, than he did. And, strangely, that forced us apart. Our relationship ended about the same time he lost the general election to Cal Mabry, the Anglo, Republican opponent.

Part of our topsy-turvy situation was Rudy's belief that I could be of some help to his campaign, help in getting the Anglo vote. "Any Mexican-American dating an Anglo woman would be worth us voting for"—that kind of logic is what he assumed. He would introduce me to strangers at the most ridiculous times: "This is my friend Alta Kay Dunsmore, out here from Illinois." What did they care about me, about Rudy, about us? He had no sense of decorum, none whatsoever. And when we would see a Hispanic couple, and I would encourage him to acknowledge them, he would excuse himself, leave me standing there, and go over and greet them in Spanish: "Buenas noches. Que tal?" How was I supposed to feel? I soon gave up on it. It was a hopeless relationship, at least in public.

Oh, we had some good times. Especially on weekends at the rodeo out on Arenal Road, off of Coors. He would do the announcing. Really had a nice voice. "And next, ladies and gentlemen, is the bareback bronc competition. Hold on to your cinches!" And because of his square dance calling, he could holler, "Ah haaa" with the best of them—sing it, really.

I would sit in the stands, drinking a cherry soda or an RC, with my scarf tied tight around my head and the little gritty pieces of sand in my teeth from all the rodeoing and gusts of mesa wind. And I would listen to the PA speakers and watch the kids playing and running for the snack bar. I would thrill to the power and bucking of the horses and the determination of the riders—all kinds of riders, all kinds of people: Anglo, Indian, Hispanic. I just thoroughly enjoyed the strangeness and the spectacle of it all. The West! These were not Illinois farmers off for a livestock auction, for big dray horses, for dairy cows. Car horns would honk, cheers would go up. It was great fun.

One Saturday Rudy entered the calf-roping event. He borrowed Billy Harper's big bay quarter horse, Bud, and put up the fifteen-dollar entry fee, and said it would be good publicity. It should have been worth doing just for the doing. But Rudy always had some kind of campaign strategy involved, ever ambitious.

Anyway, he looked majestic, sitting there behind the gate on old Bud. You could see the hat, of course, the big-brimmed white straw hat. You could see he had the piggin' string in his mouth, and then the calf was out of the chute and the gate flew open and Bud jumped after the calf, almost leaving Rudy on the fence. But he not only held on, he had the lariat swinging over his head, faster and faster, and the big rippling legs of the horse were closing in on the calf. And you could hear the sounds of the man and the horse and the calf—the bawling and the breathing and the thunder of Bud's big hooves in the dust. And then, then the rope reached out across the blue sky and caught the calf around the neck and Bud put on the brakes, stiffening his rear legs and holding hard with his rear haunches till the rope tightened, pulling the poor calf up short, flipping it back on the ground.

Then Rudy was off Bud and running for the struggling, bawling calf, guiding himself along the rope. With all his strength he reached over the calf and threw it down, grabbing its legs and taking the piggin' string from his mouth and securing first one front leg, then the other three, and throwing his arms high in the air to signal the timer. And hitting his hat, knocking it off into the sand, announcing to all his baldness. And you could tell, it got to him, deflated him, diminished him.

It was too damn bad. Too shitty bad that he just couldn't be less self-conscious. His time wasn't the best—forty-two seconds. But for me, then, it was a triumph. At that point I was starting to love the guy. What the hell difference did it make that he was bald? I didn't care. He cared. It was a revealing moment. And it changed our whole relationship.

Billy Harper could tell, too. He had come up to sit by me. And that was fine. It added to the fun because he filled me in about Bud, about what a good roping horse he was and how he knew just how to work. But Billy was watching my responses too and saw me flinch when Rudy wilted without the protective powers of his hat, probably heard me say, "Damn it, Rudy" or some such words of disappointment.

Billy, being who he was, moved in and for the first time in a really conscious way I thought about him sexually. It was fleeting, but when he reached out in my own disappointment and put his arm around me, saying, "Too bad," just as they announced Rudy's time, I felt the vibes, knew what he was really saying.

Funny how one little thing, one little action or disappointment can cap off a whole series of events, allow you to see deep into a person's character and know it just won't be, the two of you just won't make it.

So when Rudy made his way over to us I pretty much knew. Billy congratulated him and laughed, calling him a real cowboy. They shook hands. And Rudy bragged about Bud. What a fantastic horse he was. Billy asked us to meet him for beers after the final event. We agreed.

Then Rudy gave me a kiss on the cheek and did himself in. "Will you hold this for a second?" and handed me his white straw hat while he bent down to take off his spurs. Just then a big gust of wind hit, off the mesa, forming the whirling funnel of a dust devil. "Oh, . . . oops," I said as I released Rudy's hat, watching it climb upward over the stands in the company of empty potato chip sacks, trampled rodeo fliers and old campaign posters.

BLUE DANUBE WALTZ

AFTER MY FIRST AUDITION, MISS MATTHEWS SAID, "WE WILL BEGIN with volume two in the Nick Manoloff series. It is available at May's Music Store downtown. I believe that's where you purchased your instrument, according to the bradded company logo on your case. You are clearly beyond the beginner stage, and yet . . . and yet you are not truly at the intermediate stage. The second volume of Mr. Manoloff's plectrum method should suit just fine. Your first lesson will be next Wednesday at 7:00 P.M. Please be prompt, Gilbert. We haven't much time."

I had dreaded meeting Miss Matthews. There were a lot of stories about her. Living the way she did. All her dogs. Her shack of a house. She wasn't at all like Jerry. So what if he was an alcoholic? So what if he showed up drunk for my lesson? But that's not what my mother said. "No nightclub derelict is giving my son guitar or any other kind of lessons. Not in my house. Not anywhere!" She really got on her high horse, "threw a royal fit," to use the words my father always used when his "old lady" was upset.

As for Miss Matthews, it hadn't been as bad as I had thought it would be when my brother first parked in front of her decrepit little house on Gatewood. But I was eager for him to pick me up and, because of the reflection in the front window, had noticed him turn into the drive, hit the small ravine by her mailbox, and then cut the headlights, turn on the parking lights and wait in the red glow of a cigarette and, I knew for certain, the country music sounds of KOAT. He too had said, "Don't make me wait."

As I placed my guitar back in its case and said my good-byes I was more than ready to leave, although my fears had died down somewhat. The place really was shabby, outside, even in the dark. On the way across the yard I tripped on a big dog chain. Inside, the place was musty. Lots of overstuffed chairs and a big sofa with a bedspread over it. All in one small room—dominated by an ornately crafted, oak-cased, upright piano, with "Baldwin" naming it in gold decals. The floor was bare wood, with footpaths worn in it and with just one special carpet, a pretty Persian-looking one, under the piano bench. Her two dogs, a big collie-shepherd cross with a matted coat and a short-haired terrier of some kind, stayed in the kitchen. She wore at least two sweaters over her blouse and a long skirt that looked like it was made out of the same material as the curtains tied back and away from the front window.

Everything in the house smelled a bit mildewed. The house needed airing. And she did too. She was pale. She seemed almost totally colorless. The room and its furnishings seemed colorless too—except for the piano. And except for the last remnants of red in her graying hair. You could still tell that when she was young her hair had been red, or strawberry blond.

Closing the case, I noticed again the crack spreading out laterally from the end pin. Only a fraction of a fraction of an inch. I couldn't be sure how far. Couldn't really measure its marching advance. But its progress was inevitable—always there, bothering me, haunting me. Like death and the final coffin closing.

One moment of frustration. A slam of the instrument to the floor, driving the white plastic plug into the soft mahogany wood was all it took. A small, hairline crack at first. Then it started spreading. Then a major, visible crack.

Miss Matthews hadn't said anything about the crack when she had picked up my guitar and examined it, running her bony, big-veined hands with their tissue-paper skin across the strings, listening intently as they vibrated over the round sound hole, holding up the instrument to the light, cradling it in her lap. "This instrument is adequate, Gilbert," was all she said. She saw the scratches around the sound hole and beneath the half-moon, tortoiseshell pick guard. She saw the end-pin crack. She heard the difference it made. She had an ear for such things. Had to notice. Had to hear. She only frowned slightly, hesitated almost imperceptibly.

I hadn't told anybody about that crack. Not even Jerry. Not when it happened. Not when I first noticed it spreading slowly up and around the body, running with the grain of the wood, threatening to split the whole sound box and destroy the instrument. Render it dead in two useless pieces. "Hey, when did you crack your axe, Gillie? Better fix it" was all Jerry said. He saw it right away. But to repair it would announce its existence. Certainly I couldn't tell my father and mother. They had worked hard to put aside the $109 to buy the instrument, plus an extra $25 for the soft-shell case. Three dollars for the orange-and-black rope cord put on the guitar personally—neck nut to end pin—by Bernie May himself. Another dollar for polish. Both of them had gone with me, straight to Mr. May, to select just the right guitar for their boy, destined, they hoped, for a Decca or an RCA recording contract with the likes of the Tennessee Plowboy, Eddy Arnold.

"How do you like it, son? It's a beauty. Take good care of it and it will take you far. Could make you a fortune," beamed my father, and turned to shake hands with Mr. May.

"Oh, Gillie, you will practice hard, won't you?" chimed in my mother. "Early morning is the best time. When your mind is fresh and alert."

"That's right, my boy. Thirty minutes each day, minimum, and one day we'll be selling your records right here in this very store. Have your picture on the wall like those artists over there." And Mr. May pointed to glossy photographs of wide-hatted Western singers with their names signed across their guitars: "To Bernie," "Thanks, Bernie," "Best regards, Bernie," "Your pal." It was endless and impressive. Picture after picture after picture. Plus promotional posters! And the guitar was so beautiful in its newness and promise. Not a scratch on it. Not a blemish. The aroma of spruce top, rosewood neck, pearl dot inlay frets, soft-white purfling, glistening sunburst lacquer. I would practice. I would. People in cars, at home, in music stores would hear me.

Lessons with Jerry had been pretty easy. He showed me how to hold the guitar. Showed me how to crook my finger and place my thumb on the pick—the right size and thickness. Showed me some chords, wrote out some lyrics, to tunes like "Foggy River," "Anytime," "The Wabash Cannonball," "Tennessee Waltz." Showed me with penciled letters C, F, G or D, G, A when to change positions. It was fun. He would bring out his guitar and strum a few chords, do some fancy runs high up on the neck, and then pretty much go through some of the tunes he knew. He never insisted that I practice or anything like that. We just played some tunes together. Then he would light up a smoke and hang around for a cup of coffee and the $2.50 he charged for thirty-minute lessons.

But Miss Matthews was going to be more demanding. I could tell that as soon as I bought Nick Manoloff's *Guitar Method, Vol. II.* There he was on the cover, his hair slicked back—and he wore a tuxedo. Can you believe it? A tie-and-tails kind of guy. And the tunes in the book had names like "Over the Waves," "Long, Long Ago," "Volga Boat Song," things like that. There were scales for all the positions and all the keys and a bunch of notes and key signatures and foreign words. My folks wanted me to be like Eddy Arnold, not all the obscure guys whose pictures offered testimonial on the title page to Nick Manoloff and his stuffed-shirt guitar method.

When I handed it to Miss Matthews, she turned right away to two tunes pretty far into the book: "Denka Waltz" and one that went on for two or three pages—"The Blue Danube Waltz." Then she folded the book back so it would stay on her piano and started playing. Then she started singing some words to "The Blue Danube Waltz," all from memory, I guess. She really got carried away. Almost forgot I was there—playing her piano, singing along to this song I had never heard or heard about! Her back arched. She closed her eyes and pointed her face to the ceiling and didn't even look at the book after a bit. I was pretty uncomfortable. Then she stopped playing and sat silent for a moment, coming back from wherever she had been.

"We will play this as a duet, young man. It will be our goal. If you learn to play this you will always find enjoyment in your guitar. And you will be able to better understand other songs. I will teach you to play this song with feeling, as if you were dancing abroad to the orchestral arrangements of the immortal Strauss. Mr. Manoloff and I will usher you into the world of beauty, into the transportations of purist rhythm and melody. You will be caressed and refreshed in the waters of the Blue Danube."

I didn't know quite what to think. She was strange. Old Gene Laferink's mother, who had recommended Miss Matthews to my mother as a guitar teacher, had said that much. And Gene had confirmed it too, though he called her "wacky." The song, "Blue Danube Waltz," looked much beyond my skill level. Jerry had taught me some technique, I guess, but I was compelled to blurt out, "But I don't know how to read music."

"No mind, you will," was her reply, and we began that very night to supplement Mr. Manoloff's intermediate method book with lessons of Miss Matthews's own devising. When I asked why I couldn't play "Tennessee Waltz" or something like that instead, she simply stared at me with an expression of high disdain.

The routine began to take on a familiarity. My brother would drop me off and then pick me up, always waiting while she wrote out the next week's assignment. He would commiserate with me. And slowly we started making it, page after page, closer and closer to "Blue Danube Waltz." The fear of not practicing soon replaced the fear about the cracked condition of my guitar. I became friends with both of her dogs, who would come to greet me at the door and then retire back to their corner as my lesson began.

"Denka Waltz" came and went as first I accompanied her and then she accompanied me, each of us taking turns playing the melody and then chording. And there were some pretty difficult chords too, full-voiced chords, extended chords.

"Wonderful, Gilbert. We are almost to the Danube. Almost ready to cross."

That moment came early in October. She assigned "Blue Danube Waltz." And she prefaced it by saying, "This is what we have been working for. This is the song I wish you to play in next month's recital of my best students. We will play a duet!" I had to admit I had come to like some of Nick Manoloff's tunes—his arrangements for guitar and all. So I started working on the "Danube." We worked it out in three or four sections, learning one and then another, and then putting them all together. My fingers and wrists were stronger than they had ever been. Lessons were running longer and longer, forty-five minutes, an hour.

My brother rebelled and other family members had to pick me up—usually one of my parents or an aunt; even Willis Debke was enlisted one evening. Finally Miss Matthews judged me almost ready for the recital and, after nearly a year of study and practice, I did have "The Blue Danube Waltz" under technical control. "You still must feel the spirit of the song more deeply, Gilbert. Take your guitar to the river and play to the waters that dance about you. Imagine that water is not the brown, dirty water of the Rio Grande, but the rich, wonderful, blue water of the Danube."

I tried that. Walked about a mile down Bridge Street, and then down the big drainage ditch by La Vega Road, finally crossing through the bosque to the Rio Grande. I felt mainly the sand and the cracked clay and the pungent aroma of Russian olives and watched the shimmer of cottonwood leaves. Saw the sunlight glisten on the churning water.

My fingers knew all the notes, all the complicated chords. But I realized that I could never really feel the spirit of "The Blue Danube Waltz." What I felt was the spirit of the great river, the mighty Rio Grande, the water of my birthplace, coursing from Colorado head-waters through Texas and into the Gulf of Mexico. Rather than sorrow at some great loss, some embarrassment to Miss Matthews, I felt joy in realizing what I really felt—my river, my soul—and I played, instead, all the early songs Jerry had taught me, now embel-lished, to be sure, by more masterful melodic runs. I even cut loose with some Spanish tunes Rosendo Abeyta had shown me one day in the park by the zoo. I had returned to my self. Recognized and returned to my musical home, my truer songs of the heart. Strangely, Mr. Manoloff and Miss Matthews had pointed a new direction, a new route back to my past, back to what I really was, really felt. Miss Matthews was right about one thing: you had to feel your music. She felt "The Blue Danube." But I didn't, . . . didn't feel "The Blue Danube Waltz" as she could hear it—out of who knows what past European ecstasies, past my playing, past my fretting and fingering there in her small house of memories.

The recital came and went. Barcelona School's cafeteria became an auditorium of approving parents—Miss Matthews's recital, their recital, not mine. We played our Danube duet. Even in her recital dress she couldn't shed the dinginess that surrounded her. I felt a tinge of sorrow, the sorrow youth has for age, as she again was transported, as she basked in the pride of parental applause.

On the ride home I told my parents about the crack, about the damage I had caused, frustrated in wanting to play more than I knew, more than I could. Told them that I wanted to trade guitars. Wanted a new kind of guitar, called a Fender "solid body." Told them that I couldn't really take more lessons from Miss Matthews. And that, for at least a time, I wanted to teach myself, play my own songs. Get with Gene and Rosendo and some guys at school and maybe form a little band.

"Good to hear you want to get back to the Eddy Arnold sound, son," said my father somewhat over his shoulder as he caught my eye in the rearview mirror.

"Don't worry about the crack to the guitar," volunteered my mother. "We can trade it in for something even closer to Eddy Arnold's. Mr. May will show us which one, I'm sure. He has photos of all the stars. But your duet was so pretty. And that waltz, that 'Blue Danube,' I liked it."

"Have you heard of Carl Perkins?" I asked, looking ahead in the street to see if we would make the traffic light, ". . . and a tune called 'Blue Suede Shoes'?"

KIMO

IT STRUCK ME AGAIN, SEEING HIM STRETCHED OUT ON THE STAIN-less-steel operating table, with the tube down his trachea, how much he looked like a lion. The blond coat, the massive head and powerful shoulders, were what led me to call him Kimo.

It's a Tewa word I learned from Frank Sangre, an Isleta Indian who used to take me deer hunting on the reservation close to Los Lunas. Early one morning a puma, resting on a scrub-oak ledge, gazed down at us, and Frank just said, "Kimo" and kept on walking.

I followed fast behind him, holding my breath, and, between glances at the rocky trail to keep my footing, I turned to stare back at the majestic creature.

"I've just about got it," Wayne said and put down the pin-chuck handle and mallet to reach inside. Kimo's left hip was opened, muscle peeled back, bone and cartilage glistening through the blood. *Sangre* means "blood," I thought, again marveling at Frank's long-ago introduction to the puma.

Wayne was no ordinary small-town veterinarian. We'd been partners about two years before I really realized, watching him work on Kimo, what a good surgeon he was.

"Maybe we better take this guy up to Fort Collins for this kind of work," was my first reply when Wayne suggested we try to make a "new dog" out of Kimo.

"Relax, partner. I know a horse doctor like you isn't use to such complex procedures. But believe me, it's a piece of cake."

It wasn't, of course. Trying to fix hip dysplasia on a young golden retriever surgically has its risks. But Wayne saw it as a challenge and quipped, "I owe it to a dog who looks so much like a cat."

So, amid my boyhood memories of mountain lions and Pueblo hunting trips, Wayne repositioned tendon and muscle, stitched up Kimo's hip, and switched off the anesthetic and the overhead lamps.

Within weeks Kimo was jumping into my pickup and we were on the gravel farm roads, making the rounds throughout Doña Ana County.

To make it as a veterinarian in New Mexico you almost have to treat large animals. I don't mean really large animals like a vet for a zoo deals with. I mean farm animals—cattle, horses, sheep, swine. At Colorado State University, where I received my D.V.M., I did get the chance to watch some frantic work to relieve sand colic in a buffalo kept in captivity and used in advertising by a local car dealer. That's as exotic as it ever got. When I went through the program at State the curriculum was directed toward livestock, not animal welfare.

If you set up business as a vet here in the hinterland, you just expect to treat farm animals. Period. Sure, you get some dogs and cats in our little clinic, located as it is on the edge of town, where the land starts to turn into the flat, rich space of pecan groves and cotton fields. But the arrangement was—in the days before Kimo—I was to take all the country calls and Wayne would treat town animals.

He was interested in "pets" and who owned whom. Compassion. Psychology. That sort of thing. At the time I wasn't. I was strong enough to deliver a calf or a foal, tough enough to be satisfied with just a local anesthetic, unfazed by the squeals of serial hog castration.

Elsie Baca, our bookkeeper and expert pet groomer, took all the calls and made all the appointments, handled the business side of it and even advised on tax-sheltered annuities. That was before Kimo, too. But what happened to Kimo in the end changed me deeply— gave me a different sense of purpose.

Now I see my work and our clinic in a much broader perspective. Now, treating animals is much more than a dollar-and-cents equation, or even a profession. It's a calling and I'm zealous about it. Never thought it would happen to me, but when Kimo died I came to new feelings about the meaning and values all animals really have, came to resist seeing the animal kingdom divided into either food or friendship or finances.

Wayne is a better surgeon now than when he fixed Kimo's hip. I've marveled at what he's done to bring animals back from very probable deaths. Wayne, or I, the whole school of veterinary medicine at State couldn't have saved Kimo from the death that awaited him. The causes were large ones, interconnected with all of the dumb, brutish attitudes society holds about animals. Most of the surgery Wayne does is routine—clipping the ears of a schnauzer, declawing cats. Testing for leukemia. Giving shots—and advice. He tries to keep his preference for cats to himself.

Maybe once a year someone from town will bring in a wayward raccoon, or an injured squirrel or skunk, or even a fledgling robin. I didn't understand all the emotion some people have about pets— before Kimo. I've not yet come to the point where *only* animals matter. I can see how you might be driven to that. But you can't take humans out of the equation. Out of his agony and death Kimo pointed the way for me.

There's a story involved with every "customer" we bill, every animal we treat, every person we laugh with or console. Some of the stories reveal just how many damn fools there are in the world. Some of the stories, as you come to know them, imagine them, or fill them in around the edges, damn near break your heart. You do have to keep a balance between getting too sappy and too distanced from it all. But somewhere, especially these days, you can't help getting philosophical about it—what animals have meant and could mean.

My own story, my life and times with Kimo, my great-hearted retriever, puts some of the bigger picture in focus for me: the fervent interdependency of animals and people and the unbelievable disregard and callousness of some people—even veterinarians like me.

I mean, attention must be paid to what's at the very core of human perceptions of *living* animals, not the *fallacies* of pets in cartoons and stereotypes, animated or otherwise. Attention must be paid to issues about leather and fur products, the beef and pork industry, to animal experimentation, to trapping—these big, volatile issues that turn serious and explosive fast.

Kimo was a part of my life when I was the dumb animal. Not him. Call this story a testimonial if you wish, to a dog who meant the world to me and would still be alive today had he not accidentally collided with a Conibear #330 kill trap. Here's to Kimo, who allowed me to see a bit beyond slogans about "man's best friend," allowed me to really know an animal.

For me, "Hey, David," were the first words in Kimo's story. Wayne said them over a cup of coffee in our file-cabinet lounge.

"Elsie and I admitted Snipes's lame pup today while you were out at Anderson's. Snipes said he just couldn't afford more costs. Bad dysplasia in one hip. Want to take a look? Hate to put it away. He's a chunky guy—pretty as a big cat."

That's how it started. Dysplasia is common enough in retrievers; goldens and labradors often have it. And they shouldn't be bred, really, if they do. Weakens the whole line. Most good breeders are careful about that. But this one was here in our clinic. And he was a great-looking pup. Aside from some pain and problems walking and sitting, he was healthy. Little doubt that it was a purebred dog. And Wayne was right. The big blond head definitely made this dog look like a lion.

So I reached back in my Isleta past and named him Kimo. Wayne thought the name had something to do with Tonto and the Lone Ranger—all that stereotyped "The trail leads this way, kemo sabe" talk. Anyway, Wayne started calling me Tonto and fixed Kimo's hip with some razzle-dazzle cutting and chiseling. And before long the darn dog could actually jump into the cab of my pickup and was staring out the window at the pecan orchards, sniffing at the rural air, barking at the hogs and wagging his monster tail for all the farm kids.

Pheasant season was a short but enjoyable time for me even before I had Kimo. I had no qualms about hunting. Kimo took naturally to hunting upland game. He would tire a little faster than another dog his age would. His hip was strong, but the constant pull of mud in a slough bottom or walls of thick bosque brush would take their toll. Sometimes after a turn or two I would have to lift him into the pickup. Too tired to jump. But there were more than enough birds to make our forays short, and I was careful in pacing him.

For a couple of seasons everything was fine. Then I made the mistake of hunting some county land near Hatch just above Mesilla. It was a crisp Saturday morning early in November. Near the Santa Fe tracks I had seen a covey of quail fly into some river cover. And so I marked it for me and Kimo to hit early some morning.

That morning came. It was a fateful one. Kimo was out of the truck in a flash, smelling every errant odor and aroma he could. Frisky. Alive. We walked down the tracks for a short distance and then veered north, along the fence row just on the edge of the bosque. Kimo crossed under the fence, and I kept walking on the track side of the fence. He picked up a scent, and his tail started whipping like wiper blades on my Chevy in a rainstorm. I was feeling good, filled with great pancakes and eggs from Josie's Cafe.

And then, in a flash, in side vision I saw Kimo go down, heard the terrible yelps and growls. His lion's head was held to the ground and then his whole body was stretched out and his hip, the one Wayne had so perfectly reconstructed, was jerking and its spastic leg and foot were kicking the grass and leaves. I was over the fence and with him in a matter of seconds. A rusted Conibear kill trap was engulfing him, snapped shut around his twisted, turned neck, choking him, closing out the morning's golden sunlight and cool air. His neck was broken and bleeding and his beautiful full head was covered by the boxy, square steel rods of the ugly contraption. Raccoon tracks were plentiful and the trap box, with its two sinister side-coiled springs, had jumped on Kimo.

I couldn't pry it open—tried to use my gun barrel to free him. The noise and frenzy were pure madness. I pulled and pried and tried to talk Kimo calm. It was futile.

By the time I picked him up in the trap he was dead and gone. But I wouldn't realize it even when I laid him in the back of the truck and floorboarded it for the clinic. Racing with me were images of Sangre, of the majestic reclining puma, flashes of Wayne's confident, bloody hands restoring Kimo to what turned out to be an all-too-short life of health and wholeness. And there was the imagined face of the person who, oblivious to it all, had set the Conibear that killed Kimo.

Even now the ghost visage of that unknown trapper resembles me. Even then I knew the outlines of my expiation, outlines striving to focus a stainless-steel operating table, a simple but sinister and rusted assembly of steel rods and the sleeping but dead golden warmth and motion of an animal, of Kimo.

FIRST HORSES

SHE SAT AT THE END OF THE RED-TOPPED, CHROME-TRIMMED CAFE counter, stirring the thickest bowl of chili he had ever seen. It didn't look like the usual Bronco Cafe chili, with pieces of beef and cloves of garlic and succulent pinto beans floating in a greasy broth.

He liked to eat Bronco chili with cheese on top and with plenty of crackers washed down by a fountain Coke with three squirts of syrup and agitated by carbonated water shot hard into the ice and concentrated Coke—and whatever other syrups whose handles he hit.

In front of the girl's business-issue crockery bowl was a ribbed-plastic glass still full of water. No ice. Next to that, resting on a small plate, and drooping over the edges, was a piece of still-steaming Indian bread.

Florinda was the girl's name, as he heard it, for the introduction was fast, since Lucy did the honors: "Gilbert, this is Florinda. Florinda Tenaja. She's from Isleta. She's the new waitress. First day!"

The boy, out of school for the afternoon, with books and notebooks in hand, and just through the side door of the cafe, stopped—politely, but still thinking about history class—and stood by the end of the counter looking at the girl and her meal.

Further down the counter sat Abrán, in his usual place, making the moves on Lucy during one of his frequent breaks from his brother's body and fender shop across the street. Reuben, Abrán's brother, was a cheerful guy, always clowning. Abrán was different. He was silent, sullen, as if he were mad at himself—maybe mad at his thinning hair and almost bald head, maybe mad at his one-horse shop and at . . . "todo el mundo, ese." He liked to talk with Lucy, usually in low, Latin-lover whispers—and with one intense purpose.

One time the boy had come into the darkened cafe at closing time and found Abrán and Lucy behind the counter kissing. Her thin, synthetic-blend uniform skirt was pulled up around her waist, and the boy remembered Abrán's dark, calloused hands holding Lucy through her pink underwear. Abrán's hand now raised a cup of black coffee to his lips as he half turned his head and, with his still steely stare, acknowledged the boy with a look that glowered all the way back to that twilight interruption months in the past, maybe even back to the Mexican War and Colonel Kearny's invasion.

"Qué dice, Abrán? How's it going, man?" the youth almost yelled, with as much bravado and authentic Spanglish pronunciation as he could muster.

"Hola, Mendigo Gilbert," was Abrán's cutting reply.

Then, turning nervously, with feigned interest, to the new girl, the boy said, "Hello, nice to meet you"—rote words accompanying his preoccupied look again at the girl's rich, orange-red bowl of chili with its cleavered chunks of meat and a base more the texture of morning Cream of Wheat than *his* kind of chili, the Bronco's kind of chili, the greasy-filmed cafe chili that he ate out of a soul-hunger as strong and ravishing as Abrán's longing for Lucy, a hunger that even now he could sense in Abrán's leaning across the counter and, with those same large, remembered dark hands, holding his cup out for a refill of "mud" and attention from *la mujer,* from "wisa."

A quiet "Hi" was Florinda's answer to the youth, and she slowly lowered her head and began stirring again, with the large, tarnished cafe spoon, the pieces of meat in the bowl—back and forth, back and forth. There was no garlic. There were no beans—only the creamed, orange-red chili with small, hard, yellowish pod seeds coursing to the top.

She was Indian for sure. Probably a couple of years older than Gilbert. Maybe seventeen or eighteen. Short-cropped black hair. Round dark face. Bright brown-black eyes. He noticed too that her blue and white apron was embroidered in Isleta fashion, in closely stitched navy-blue thread, with delicate miniature horses, little Indian ponies, blocked and squared and stylized.

There was at once an ancient and a modern look, a timelessness about them—primitive, compelling: steeds from out of the annals of the Crusades and the epic deeds of knights questing, or jousting for a fair maiden's honor; horses from over the vast and rolling sands of Arabia; mounts heading west from Veracruz to Tenochtitlán or up the Great River with the conquerors Oñate and Coronado, and other latter-day vaqueros and caballeros; ponies on the great American plains in pursuit of bison or the counting of coup; wild mountain mustangs, roaming proudly; thoroughbred racers galloping with sweaty, shimmering muscles for the finish line at the state fair; quarter horses in rodeo regalia; stalwart workers pulling a travois across dusty miles or turning a grindstone at a picturesque riverside *molino de glorieta*.

These little horses struck the boy hypnotically as quintessential, as essences rendered in the artistry of thread. Across the top of the bib of her apron was an elaborate edging of black thread, bridled and harnessed and controlling. It was a beautiful apron compared to Lucy's worn, food-stained smock, apparel that looked more like a grease-spattered dishtowel than anything else.

Seated there in her Indian apron, Florinda Tenaja wasn't anything like Lucy. Not beautiful and alluring—able to flirt and follow through with even the toughest of the cruel teasers, like Abrán, or the more benevolent ones, like C. V. Hankle and O. D. Schmidt, the two owners of C&O Motors down the street. No doubt her social trial by fire (hotter than Hatch chili), with the whole gaggle of regular customers, had come earlier in the day over all the Anglicized menu of dishes: maybe at breakfast over ham and eggs and chili verde; maybe over mid-morning Farmer Brothers coffee and doughnuts; and at noon over meat loaf and mashed-potato plate lunches, topped off with oversized pieces of Jill's Bakery pecan pie à la mode. Such was the boy's imagined guess.

Now the girl was on a late-afternoon break. Buddy Tedrick, with his Buick Roadmaster, his eye patch, and his Forrest Tucker good looks, was due about this time every afternoon. One of the reasons the boy liked the Bronco after school was because of Buddy, "Tooter," they called him because of the assembly of horns on his Roadmaster.

He had taken a couple of air horns off wrecked semis as they came into the junkyard and mounted them, replated and gleaming, on his car. Then he had some musical-sounding horns under the hood, which played a three-note doorbell chime that he used as a finale. He even had a miniature siren rigged up to scare other drivers and pedestrians at special times. His car was spectacular: canary-yellow, red-leather upholstery, white top with a small isinglass rear window, four chrome portholes on each fender, and a couple of glasspack mufflers that could purr or growl depending on how much boot he gave the accelerator. Everybody liked Tooter—and his car.

From the first top-down ride in the Buick around the valley and across the Rio Grande bridge, Gilbert had wanted to be like Tooter. He knew what to say and when to say it—and he played lead guitar, a big blond Gibson L-5, with the Manzano Mountain Boys, out at the Paradise Inn in Tijeras Canyon, at the Palomino Club on Coors Road, and, every third Saturday night, at the rowdiest of all the town's cowboy clubs, the Hitching Post farther out on West Central at the edge of the volcanoes. He had even been on local radio shows, and talk had it straight from Tooter that the band might even land a weekly television show with KOB, the NBC "affiliate," to quote Tooter's new radio lingo and voice.

He was a good friend, and lots of laughs, a guy with "person-ality." Gilbert wanted to line up some guitar lessons once he bought a guitar. He was always talking with Tooter about guitars. Gilbert knew how to talk with Tooter. But the new girl would need all the strength of her meal for her first meeting with Tooter and for his razzle-dazzle, drugstore-cowboy charm.

Still thinking about Tooter, in his happy after-school tones the boy spoke: "Hey, Loosie Lucy, how about my Bronco burger like I like 'em? Make it stud. And a bowl of beans and red?" came his usual afternoon incantation.

"Wish and command," responded the waitress. "One Bronco. Make your own suicide Coke, cowboy," and she grabbed a generous patty of meat out of the whale-size Norge, peeled off the waxed paper, and tossed the red slab on the sputtering double grill. When she reached up to get the spatula to press the raw hamburger meat to the hot metal, he stared at the outline of her bra strap underneath her waffle-weave nylon/rayon/orlon uniform, and marveled at her full, heavy breasts and outlined nipples, and quickly glanced down at her legs showing long and smooth and bare beneath the elevated uniform hem.

Amid his reveries and wonderment at the memory of her standing behind the counter in Abrán's hands Gilbert knew something else—Abrán was luckier than Lucy. And probably Buddy was just as lucky if not luckier than Abrán. Buddy flirted like crazy with Lucy. Maybe it was the competition with Abrán more than the desirability of Lucy, but one look at her disproved that theory. Buddy was 100 percent better than Abrán in the boy's book, and he sensed too that Abrán and Buddy only pretended to be friends.

When she turned her head away from talking to Abrán to speak to him, at first he couldn't believe that he heard Lucy say, "Want some, kid? . . . Want some of Flora's chili? She just made it. Plenty of chili. Plenty of flour. Plenty of *carne*. Light on the water! Get it while it's hot . . . and it's hot, *c-a-l-i-e-n-t-e,* HOT. Jalapeño/Japaleno hot! Think you can handle it? She made some Indian bread too. Beats a horse burger."

Brought partially out of his reveries, Gilbert replied, "You bet. Give me a bowl. Nothing's too hot for a chili champ—prince of the pintos. Let me at it," he blared as he put his notebooks on the shelves over the wooden crates of bottled soft drinks—the Nehi, the Orange Crush, the RC, the Cokes—and walked behind the counter.

"Still go with the burger, and Indian bread and honey for dessert," Gilbert continued, and looked over at Florinda and smiled.

He took down a large Coca-Cola glass with the white script letters scrawled across the bulged-out top, and with his back turned to the counter he looked into the mirror behind the shelf of clean glasses to catch the Indian girl's eyes looking at him—eyes that seemed tired as much as anything, but frightened and forlorn too, sad and injured in isolation, eyes that seemed to look at him and beyond him and his strange familiarity and belonging behind this chrome-and-red counter, not yet claimed by her; beyond, much beyond the mirror's reflection of the cars moving back and forth on the pavement in front of the cafe, on the street that ran south all the way to Isleta and Los Lunas and Belen, or northeast, just across the bridge, to downtown—the street that Gilbert loved to cruise with Buddy, the street that would bring the bus to the next corner, in front of old man Terrell's Variety Store, later that evening, to take her back down Isleta Road, sixteen miles to the reservation and the pueblo. Where she belonged—or used to.

Lots of Isletans worked off the reservation—for the railroad in Belen and in Albuquerque; on the *Doodlebug,* which ran back and forth between the two railroad towns; on the military bases sprawling at the foot of the Manzano Mountains. Long known as the ancient hunting grounds of the pueblos and protected as their exclusive domain, Hell's Canyon and much of the other reservation mountain land was now bordered by Manzano Base and Sandia Weapons Center, the next links in Los Alamos Laboratory's atomic bomb supply chain, the much-rumored but still secret high-security assembly line and storehouse for more advanced brothers and cousins of "Little Boy" and "Fat Man" and their awesome hunger for destruction.

Old "I-Like-Ike" had alluded to the bases and their contribution to national defense and the growing "military-industrial complex" on his campaign stop in Gallup at the Indian Ceremonial. The boy remembered the words and the white convertible and Eisenhower in a corny headdress, making "How—Me Indian. Me Like Ike" signs in front of the El Rancho Grande Hotel, and waving to everybody along both sides of the parade route like they were troops celebrating victory in Europe.

The location and name of Hell's Canyon in the Manzanos now took on a new kind of irony, and Isleta was now a modern "island" of a new kind, little anticipated by the Spanish conquerors who named it—an island situated on longitudes and latitudes between the barbarism of wars past, present, and to come.

The pueblo women who left the reservation worked in town stores as clerks or as housekeepers and waitresses, like Florinda. Now and then young Isletans would turn up in the public schools. Gilbert knew one or two in his school. Lorenzo Jojolla was in his homeroom. Many more pueblo kids from up and down the Rio

Grande Valley and over in Navajo land went to the Indian School north of town. There they had room and board and could learn a trade and explore Central Avenue in courageous scouting expeditions to the El Rey and the Cortez, the Sunshine and the Kimo. There they could eat popcorn, watch Hollywood cowboys that looked a lot like Tooter ride horses, kill Indians, and shoot up the glorious, gory frontier in Saturday-afternoon, black-and-white, grade B entertainment. There, on the screen during the feature and during the *March of Time* newsreels they could learn and relearn their place in history.

Gilbert wasn't anywhere close to thinking about the larger implications of history—world or Eastern, American or Western. He liked his class in U.S. history. At least he recognized that much. He recognized too that as he looked at Florinda he saw her not just through the reflections of shelf mirrors and fountain Coke glasses but through the words of Mr. Marez, his history teacher, and through the anecdotes and asides of other Spanish-American friends—like Abrán and Lucy (Lucinda was her given name)—as well as Anglicized stories and myths (and jokes) told by his own family, especially his older brother, Clifford, who worked at the Covered Wagon Trading Post in Old Town and could relate an endless stream of "Yah te hey" accounts about all kinds of Indians—Navajo, Apache, Hopi, Pueblo, you name it—who came in to pawn jewelry and pottery and rugs, or trade for dry goods and other supplies.

"Hear the one about the cowboy whose truck stopped in the desert?" Clifford would ask. "Injun trouble! Get it?"

Clifford's hero was Kit Carson, of all people. In history class Mr. Marez gave a decidedly Spanish and European account of the settling of the New World, Nueva Granada, or New Spain, he called it. "The Pueblos gave the Spaniards a lot of trouble, kids, a lot of trouble," and Marez would tell about the taking of Acoma, the Sky City. And about Mexican and then American rule. Carson had his orders and good reasons with the Navajos at Bosque Redondo too, Marez explained.

"*Listos!* Bronco up and out. Chili on the counter. Off the grill and into your *estómago,*" came Lucy's announcement as she reached over the fountain to the boy—her bosom blue-veined, full and bouncy—and placed his order on the counter next to Florinda's food.

"Shoot that syrup, Gillie, and get your seat on that stool and your loving arms up to that counter. I didn't make this combo, Honeybun, for it to get cold."

Now much beyond the ritualized steps of crushed ice in glass and three squirts of Coke, one of vanilla, one of chocolate, one of root beer, he thrust forward the long black handle on the carbonated water spigot of the fountain, causing ice and water and syrup to splash out of the glass and on the young girl. She flinched, touched her shiny black bangs with a paper napkin held in her turquoise-ringed fingers, and looked up, smiling.

"Oops! Sorry!" and he pulled the fountain handle toward him to lessen the pressure. "I shouldn't do that, but I like to. Misjudged the range. Didn't think about you there, that close."

He said, "Sorry" one more time, stirred the concoction with a long iced tea spoon, and set the Coke on the counter beside Lucy's scrumptious-looking, made-to-perfection Bronco burger. Then he walked from behind the fountain, wiping both hands on a towel, and mounted the round vinyl counter stool next to the girl as if it were a nervous bronc ready to spin and buck its way out of the chutes.

She moved her still-waiting glass of water to make room for his customized Coke, scrunched into herself, and slid farther over toward the end of the counter.

He took a bite of the hamburger, the tan and toasty bun still hot and greasy, the lettuce, pickle, and tomato slices fresh and tasty and coated with generous swipes of cafe-staple mustard. Then he gulped down some of his icy drink and picked up the waiting spoon for a dive at the thick Indian chili. He filled the spoon and crammed it all, meat and thick porridgelike liquid, into his mouth. He knew immediately, even before the spoon passed his lips, that he had too much, had gone too far for a first taste. His mouth flamed open, spewing out the spoon and its cargo, and he reached rapidly, frantically, again for his Coke. He swallowed most of it before he started to feel any cool relief on his tongue and along the sides and roof of his scorched mouth.

It was the hottest damn chili he had ever tasted. Hotter than a jalapeño bitten down to the stem! His mouth was throbbing, feeling not just baked but blistered.

"What kind of chili is this? What do you put in it to make it this way?" he sputtered between gulps of Coke.

"Just Indian chili that my father raised and roasted at the pueblo," she said. "Everybody at Isleta likes my dad's chili and his Indian bread. It's not hot for me. I'm used to it, I guess. Isleta chili is the best."

"There's no damn such thing as Isleta or Indian chili," came Abrán's words from a few counter stools away. "Only Spanish chili. We developed the damn chili pepper. We invented Spanish chili in the old country and raised it down in Cruces or Hatch. Go down to the Hatch Chili Festival, *ese*. Diego Grande variety from the Jorado Farms—that's the best goddamn chili. I know my chili and, *ese,* there ain't no such thing as Isleta chili. There plain ain't no such vegetable."

Gilbert found no words to reply. And just as the girl started to say something, a loud motor rev, a truck horn blast, and then the familiar doorbell chimes announced Tooter's arrival. His glasspacks. His fanfare, all right. The front screen door of the cafe flew open to frame him and, behind him, his big white-topped convertible Roadmaster Buick. As he took off his cowboy hat and ducked under the door frame, he bellowed, "The waiting's over, people. Rooty Toot Tooter is here."

He had on his pilot-style Ray Bans over his eye patch. And a fresh white tapered Western shirt with the two top snaps undone— one of his special trademarks. He wore high-waisted "commodious" Levi's, which advertised his impressive maleness, accented by a hand-carved belt, laced in white and buckled with a big silver and gold-inlay ranger buckle, which allowed some of the tip of the belt to dangle down and off to the side, casting a suggestive shadow on his Levi's. It was one of the fanciest hand-tooled Western belts in the valley, and Gilbert subconsciously started to trace on a napkin the design of the lettering of Tooter's name dyed in yellow across the back, serif letters complemented by a yellow *T* tooled and dyed on the tops of Tooter's tan dress boots, which were invariably shined to a waxy brilliance.

As Tooter moved with loping stride across the green tile cafe floor to the counter, they followed each step with their eyes. He moved like a calf roper sliding his hand down a dallied lariat heading for a record time.

"Hey, Gillie, you old picker, plunk in a quarter in that old jukebox for 'I'm Ragged But I'm Right,' E-l on the list, and they better not have changed it. That's my theme song, buckaroo. Or punch old slick-haired Faron Young's 'Live Fast, Love Hard, Die Young.' Hell's bells, even Bob Wills's 'San Antonio Rose' or Merle Travis smokin' and strokin', feelin' and frettin' the G-string on "Wildwood Flower" would do me. Just pick out something lively there, Gillie Byrd. Cup of your best java, Lucy, my lady."

When he reached the counter, he stood over Abrán and patted him on the back, saying, "Why, if it isn't the *vecino viejo 'la luz de mi vida'.* . . . Fancy seeing you here. First cup on you? Well, if you insist."

Abrán's words sounded laced with old resentments. "Wrecked your Spee-u-wick yet, I hope, high pockets? I'm ready to pound it out for you and maybe even try to match the paint for extra dinero," came Abrán's scorching hello, accompanied now by the glissando tones of guitar runs and companion strums behind Eddy Arnold's "Don't Rob Another Man's Castle," coursing melodiously from the big red-and-yellow jukebox by the pinball machine—and augmented by a silly grin and a shrug of the boy's shoulders.

"Hey, Gillie, thanks for the song. Just what I *didn't* ask for, peckerhead. Who's your friend?" Tooter asked, ignoring Abrán for a time and giving Florinda a quick salute as he removed the curved wires of his Ray-Bans from around his ears to reveal his cool but somewhat comic black eye patch. Lucy said that Tooter had a cherry bomb explode in his face when he was a kid of eleven or twelve. Took only one eye when he reflexively jerked his head. Tooter never said anything about it to Gilbert.

"That's the new girl from Isleta," interrupted Lucy. "She's real nice. And Abrán isn't helping things by criticizing her Indian chili, her father's specialty, and her pueblo. Are you, now, Abrán?"

"I just said it's not the true chili. The Spanish brought that vegetable into this country, just like we did irrigation and everything else," came Abrán's cranky voice as he looked up at Tooter and down the counter at the Indian girl and Gilbert.

"Hell, Abrán," interrupted Tooter, "chili ain't even a vegetable. It's a fruit. And the only thing you Spanish *chapitos* brought out this way were the first horses, much as I hate to admit it. Columbus named peppers 'chili' in another naming mistake just like calling the first natives he saw 'Indians.' That's the word, ain't it, Gilberto? And don't forget VD—who's responsible for that?"

"I don't know about the first chili," offered Gilbert, "but small horses were always here, I think. And then they disappeared. First Columbus in Haiti, and then Cortés and other conquistadores re-introduced them—only eleven stallions and five mares at first, six-teen horses—when the Spanish came up from Mexico. At least that's what I remember Mr. Marez saying in history class."

"You're damn right, gringo," Abrán volunteered. "Big horses, small horses, vegetable, fruit, VD, TB, what the hell's the differ-ence? I say that the Spaniards brought the chili on their horses and showed the Isletans and all the other Indios how to plant it, irrigate it, cook it, and ride horses up and down the river and over the plains to Kansas. We even introduced sheep herding and pinto beans and tortillas and most of what holds this place together today."

"My father's people saw the first horses and the next ones the Spanish brought. We were first before the first horses," came the quiet, resolved utterance of the girl. "Isleta chili was here in the beginning, and it's the best, at least the way I fix it is."

Only the last chorus of Eddy Arnold twanging out "Don't rob another man's castle/It's written thou shalt not steal," could be heard filling the silence in the cafe.

"Put that in your hat and wear it, Abrán," said Lucy, as she walked over to the girl and reached across the counter to clear away her dishes. "Hand me your bowl of chili, honey, and hurry along now, or you'll miss your bus. That's enough hours for today."

"Believe what you will, all of you," said Abrán, as he slapped down a half-dollar, spun off the stool, and stomped toward the door and his waiting wrecked cars.

"Take off that pretty apron, Florinda, my lady," Tooter said with a smile. "Ain't no bus ride for you today. Gilbert, get your books and gobble down the rest of that Bronco burger. The three of us chili pods are off for a ride down Isleta Road. We'll outrace the bus and the

Super Chief and honk 'em hello/good-bye when we pass. I need to get me a bucket of that original hot Isleta chili."

When Gilbert turned, smiling, to look at the girl, she had untied her apron and was pulling it over her head. Then he saw the smile now breaking behind her lonesome eyes and over her whole face and reflected in the Coke glass mirror, and he understood why she held her apron, with all its herd of prancing and parading little blue stitched horses, high over her head—lingering, stretching as if exulting not just in the end of her first workday but in the strange first feeling that maybe she and the first horses had marked out a small portion of the counter and the cafe as hers.

Sensing this in a way that flashed across his Indian talks with his brother, across his history classes with Mr. Marez, and even across his strained and tense times with Abrán, Gilbert felt a bit smug, even triumphant for the first time in his life, and all he could do was wink at Lucy and say excitedly to the girl he would always insist on calling Florinda, her full name, "Well, let's go, Florinda Tenaja. Tooter's got some horses of his own, not first but fast and feisty, under that long, bright, musical yellow hood. We might even get him to put down the top and turn up the radio all the way."

"I'll see you later tonight, Lucy *mujer*," wafted back a sweetened request over Tooter's shoulder as he swept his long arms around the boy and the Indian girl and escorted them out the front door of the cafe to his beautiful Buick.

Lucy said nothing, but looked with special new feeling at each of the handsome hand-tooled letters in his belt and adjusted her bra to the tunes of Tooter's departing medley of horns and the screech of hot rubber.

LEROY

LEROY LOVED HIS HORSE AND LIVED TO RIDE HIM. THE WHOLE neighborhood knew that. We would all wave at him or call out a greeting when we saw him and Pipe. That was just about every afternoon. Anytime between three and five o'clock, there would be Leroy—riding Pipe, his blaze-faced paint pony, up Sunset Road, headed for an Eskimo Pie at Grandma Boyer's store, or back down Sunset Road, going home, trying to rein in some of Pipe's enthusiasm for the homeward trot to the horse shed behind Leroy's house. Pipe always knew when he was on his way home to the shade of his shed and his alfalfa hay. If things didn't go exactly Pipe's way, he would take the bit in his teeth and "cold-jaw" so that not even Leroy could control him.

I know, because I was riding Pipe, hanging on to the saddle straps, behind Leroy one evening when the rambunctious horse did it, over by the bridge near the old dump of a house where the Ritchies lived. Leroy had started Pipe toward home but then changed his mind and reined Pipe to the right for a turn back around the big alfalfa field to see a pelota snake. Leroy was always wanting me to see a pelota snake, said they curled up in a ball and you could roll them.

Pipe wanted nothing to do with pelota snakes, real or imagined, and he took the bit and turned back, headed in a straight line home. Leroy just gave him the reins and let him run at a full gallop. I held on for all I was worth—which I wouldn't have bet as being very much. We made it across the whole two-acre field in no time, bouncing and yelling. I could see the alfalfa whipping past around Pipe's feet, the little purple flowers and soft small green leaves crushed to smithereens.

It was frightening fun. I didn't fully understand what was going on then—just that Leroy said Pipe was showing stubborn, cold-jawing. When Pipe finally stopped and I slid off his back to the good ground, he was sweating and still skittery. Pipe wasn't more than three or four years old. He was about fifteen hands high, a good-sized horse with the stocky conformations of a quarter horse and a rather bony face, made all the more distinctive because of his black-and-white coloring.

Leroy and I had lots of adventures like that, him kidding me about pelota snakes and Gila monsters and giant horned toads. Usually we'd ride along the edge of Wiley's alfalfa field, talking and looking at things, seeing what there was to see. Our route took us by the Ritchies' house on the way to the ditch or to Boyer's. Often we would ride over and try to catch a glimpse of Wanda, Ritchie's daughter, hanging out clothes or doing chores for her old man. She would take a clothespin out of her mouth long enough to say hello to Leroy. He knew her in school at Rio Grande High.

Usually, going up Sunset Road to the store, Pipe would slough through the heavy sand along the shoulder of the road. You could see that trail almost as clearly as the one we left the day of our full-throttled ride across the trampled alfalfa. But going home from Boyer's store Pipe would really kick up the dust with his trot, iron shoes ringing in syncopated cadence on the asphalt when he broke over onto the hard surface of the road.

"It's tough to keep him from putting his head down, taking the bit, and doing what his hard head pleases. There's no stopping him then, not a chance in God's heaven," Leroy told me after our first wild ride. It wasn't so bad if Pipe cold-jawed in an open space. He could run long and free. You just prayed there were no barbed-wire fences or other barricades around.

Once in a great while Pipe would try to take the bit on the way to Boyer's store. But Leroy had the outward journey pretty much in control and coaxed Pipe along with promises of Tom's peanut butter logs from the store. They were penny candy and Pipe never got enough of, thanks to Leroy, a limitless supply. Once at the store,

Leroy would swing his leg over the saddle horn and slide off, slap the dust off his Levi's a couple of times, and then turn to Pipe and pat his neck and rub the wide white streak that ran down from his forehead to his nose and mouth. The blaze pattern flared out around the mouth to resemble a pipe bowl. So it was easy to see just how Pipe got his name. It was his natural name—named in his making. Leroy just said, "Pipe is Pipe. When she gave him to me, my aunt said, 'He's called Pipe.' "

When I rode to the store with Leroy I was always struck by the routine of the show of affection between him and Pipe. I was able to intuit clearly enough, however, just why Leroy felt so much for Pipe. Almost like Pipe, Leroy had a streak on his face too—a reddish-purple port wine stain that splotched across his left cheek from above his ear to his nose and then down the side of his neck. In rubbing Pipe's blazed face Leroy was saying something about his own birth-mark, or that's what I put together after I watched the routine two or three times.

"Good old Pipe," Leroy would say and then tie him to the barber-pole sign outside the little gray-stuccoed, tin-roofed store. And, as part of the same procedure, Leroy would adjust Pipe's bridle and joggle the side of the steel bit.

Then Leroy would say hello to whoever was in front of the store, usually old duffers waiting for John to cut their hair. His one-chair shop was little more than a room off to the side of the store, but with a window facing the main intersection where Sunset merged with Gatewood and Mesa. That's why the spot was named Five Points. John was a Spanish-American guy with a pretty thick accent. His silver-framed license over his barber chair identified him as Juan Apodaca, but he insisted we call him John. For him there was nothing worse than "chaggy" hair. So you got your money's worth when he cut your hair. He gave everyone, except Grandpa Boyer, the same haircut—kids like me and Leroy, old guys like Smitty and Mr. Mather—"short," not even the littlest bit "chaggy." Grandpa Boyer wanted some long strands left to cover his bald head. It went against John's nature, but his lease depended on it.

His finishing touch was to shave your neck and around your ears with a straight razor. He would shave an arc so high over your ears that they stood out like silly-looking mazes of skin. With Leroy you could see just how high into his hair the birthmark ran. John had a pretty illogical sign hanging from the wall, over the magazine table: "Hair Cut While You Wait!" Leroy and I would always look at the sign, give a wink and a nod, and then laugh to ourselves.

Leroy would sometimes get into pretty long conversations with people because he liked them and because everybody liked him and liked to hear what he had to say, or just liked to watch him while he listened to others talk. He was really a good-looking guy—aside from his birthmark. He was a little bit shy because of the port wine stain and the years it had colored his face and his outlook. But most of the time you just figured he forgot about the mark on his face. It bothered him too, though, you just knew it. When children would taunt him with comments like "Did you know you spilled grape juice on your face?"—such things as that—then he would clam up fast.

After a cordial greeting or two from friends around the front of the store or the barbershop, Leroy would clop up the weathered wood stairs and across the decrepit plank floor, following the footpath worn through the old gray deck paint, push open the puckered screen door with its rattletrap "Rainbow Is Good Bread" metal brace, open the noisy freezer and grab his ice cream bar, Eskimo Pie, or Fudgsicle, and stand in front of the counter or walk through the door to the barbershop or outside to the tall-handled gasoline pump, finishing his ice cream down to the last lick or two. Then he would walk over to Pipe and give him that last sweet taste of frozen treat, which Pipe would try to tongue through the heavy bit. Then would come the peanut butter candy, brown-striped and apparently very much worth Pipe's invariable whinny.

I followed them both through that routine more than once as I looked up from John's money's-worth haircuts or while I loitered around in the store absorbing neighborhood gossip or listening to the small-change sales chatter punctuated by Grandma Boyer's punching keys and pulling the handle on her ornate, filigreed cash register with all the strength her small merchant arms could muster.

Leroy was fifteen or sixteen then, I guess. I first met him about the same time his aunt gave Pipe to him for a present of some kind, maybe a birthday present or just because he was a favorite nephew.

At the time I didn't really know the full details of that story either, the big story of his aunt's motive and what Pipe was really supposed to mean to Leroy, how he was supposed to help him out. I still don't really know everything and can't truly believe what I do "know" about Pipe's sacrifice.

I know that despite his stubbornness Pipe was Leroy's friend and that Leroy was my friend. Maybe I felt some vaguely registered pity for him, the misfortune of his birthmark. But you forget about those things with friends. He liked to joke around and could tell good stories at the store and on our rides. He had a voice that always had a squeak in it at some unexpected place. My father, preoccupied with shaving, explained it to me matter-of-factly, I remember, like I should just accept nature's forces: "His voice is changing. Yours will too."

Part of the pleasure in being around Leroy, besides riding Pipe, was listening to Leroy's stories and waiting for that inevitable squeak in his voice and then the rapid, reflexive clearing of his throat that followed. It added extra suspense, not so much to what would happen next, but when it would happen. But even more interesting than his voice was his face, the port wine stain and what it did to his expressions. He was a handsome-featured guy, especially his blue-green eyes, set off against his thick, Spanish-black eyebrows and hair. His hairline ran low on his forehead and his sideburns ran long, tapering off into a kind of soft fuzziness along his lower jaw. You noticed the birthmark right away, of course—the flared-out shape and the contrasts of purple-red color, set off by his light tan complexion.

Our house was just two houses away from Leroy's, and naturally our families knew each other. I spoke to his mother when I would go by their house or when I was traipsing through yards with one of our dogs. I never saw or met Leroy's father, and nothing was ever said about him one way or the other. But I did see Leroy's aunt—his mother's sister. They were not just sisters but twins and were easy to confuse. Satherine had a more exotic look about her, wore fuller blouses and dresses. She was the kind of attractive woman you had to notice. Magnetic. The kind that made you afraid either to look or not to look.

She would turn into Leroy's driveway in her black 1947 Dodge coupe on one of her regular visits with another gift for her sister or for Leroy—or, I should say, for his horse: a saddle blanket or currycomb or some bottle of horse liniment or new piece of saddlery or tack. She also brought creams and salves and ointments for her sister, Nina, and for Leroy. For his birthmark. Sometimes his face would have a white film on it, part of the facial treatments from his "Tia Satherine." Once he even had a part dark brown, part yellow-hued liquid on his cheek. Grasshopper tobacco juice was what it looked like to me. Satherine wasn't your ordinary Watkins door-to-door representative, I could tell.

I met her once face to face, when she was getting out of her car and I had just collared my best dog, a blond spaniel called Major. In between his barks and jumps I was able to say a nervous hello to her utterance of "Ayúdame, Dios," or some such invocation, as she tried to balance several jars and bottles and close the Dodge door all at the same time.

She was a slim, somewhat emaciated woman—and tall. She always wore a big-brimmed hat or a dark-colored, soft scarf that covered her head, something like the bold-print bandanas my mother wore when she swept the cobwebs from the ceiling corners or did general housecleaning chores. It gave Leroy's aunt the look of a gypsy fortune-teller.

All of Leroy's aunt's clothes were expensive. My family insisted that she was the housekeeper of a doctor—Dr. Vaughn—over on South Fourth Street on the outskirts of the Barelas barrio. His practice was mainly people from the Country Club district but included some Barelas residents. I'm convinced now that she wasn't only a housekeeper but a nurse or a doctor of sorts too—after what happened to Leroy. He told me as much.

"Aunt Satherine is a special woman," he said, "who can see into the heart of things. She knows about herbs and medicines and has worked as a midwife for years, long before she began working with Dr. Vaughn."

One way you look at it, the day it happened wasn't so much chance or accident but destiny—something fated, arranged. Causes and convergences that come to be called "accidents" are maybe all that way. To me, at the time, it was a terrible accident, one which changed so many things—for me, for Leroy, and for Pipe.

I had seen Leroy and Pipe ride out of his front driveway and head up Sunset for the store. I waved and Leroy asked me to come along, but I had to help my parents with some gardening chores in the big irrigated plot behind our house. I was opening an irrigation gate about forty-five minutes later when I saw Pipe and Leroy coming back down Sunset. I first caught sight of them just in front of Mr. Mather's house, through some Aleanthus trees that grew along our property line. I could tell Pipe was acting up again, cold-jawing, and Leroy was having a hard time controlling him. He hadn't just given him the reins. He was fighting Pipe, trying to slow him down.

Just then old Mr. Mather pulled out of his driveway, straight in front of Leroy and Pipe, broadsiding them. The crash was loud, but for me things went into slow motion. I knew I was running and yelling for Leroy, but I couldn't really hear myself distinctly. The grill of Mather's Ford pickup knocked Pipe several feet forward onto the pavement and threw Leroy out of the saddle and into the air. He was ricocheting off the windshield back onto the hood by the time I reached the road.

Pipe was on his side, his front legs twisted and still but his back top leg kicking a little. His big body was quivering, and he tried to raise his bleeding head and whinny. But I could see he was in the final death throes and I heard his last groan resonating up from deep within his chest.

Leroy had rolled off the fender on the driver's side. Mr. Mather was dazed and rubbing his forehead and the bridge of his nose where he had collided with the steering wheel. Leroy was breathing but unconscious and bleeding from head and face cuts where he had hit and almost cracked through the windshield.

As I knelt down to try and help Leroy, I noticed that the little rivulets of his blood had started to merge and mix in the soft sand on the side of the road, following the path made by Pipe and Leroy's daily rides. Motor and radiator fluids from underneath the front end of the battered Ford were dripping there too.

People were coming out of their houses, including Leroy's

mother and aunt. I moved back as they and more expert help came, and I watched as Nina cradled Leroy's head in her lap and cried over him. Satherine stood first over Pipe, then over Leroy, crossing herself and praying. She touched Pipe's bloody muzzle, rubbing it and muttering; then she walked to Leroy, touching his face with the same hand. The pallor of Leroy's face betrayed no evidence of his former port wine stain, while Pipe's white-blazed face had reddened over with the blood of his own special death-mark.

Leroy recovered over several weeks. We would walk to the store together sometimes. He never talked about the accident. But the neighbors talked—and the cronies at the store and in John's barbershop.

"The old barbers used leeches for bleeding out impurities," John insisted.

"Sacrificial animals are as old as the Bible," Grandpa Boyer repeated.

Whether by accident or design, through trauma and fear or spiritual transfusion, everyone around Five Points agreed that Pipe had taken with him Leroy's birthmark. Mr. Mather never replaced his pickup and sat quietly in front of the store, missing Pipe almost as much as Leroy did. Satherine's visits pretty much stopped. As for me, I knew enough to keep what I knew of Satherine's part in it all a secret. But I thought of it every time I watched Leroy rub the side of his flawless face.

FIESTA

IT WAS SPRING AND FIESTA TIME. MOST OF THE SEMESTER HADN'T been a "fiesta" for us, seeing how after the fall term we were all hanging on with C's and D's. I was able to bring up just one grade to a B. That was in Professor Gribben's sociology class. I think that was his name. He was a popular professor. Didn't read from notes or anything like that. Walked around. Gestured. He kept my attention. Most of my other grades plummeted in the wake of that added effort. Whether or not I would be back as a sophomore left me in serious doubt. Things like that were the subject of Psychology 101. I lived that class. I didn't feel like I had to read about it.

You never know about the first year in college. Some guys make the grade, get on some dean's list, pledge Sigma Chi or Pikes and are on their way to becoming big man on campus with the sweetheart of this or that sorority standing right there beside them—or behind them and their egos. Most of those fraternity guys are pretty conceited. But then they have to be snobs in the circles in which they operate. I tried some of that Greek, Panhellenic stuff. Went to a rush party or two. But most of them, from my perspective, were stuck-up, just a different kind of people from what I was comfortable with. Not in sync with my "personality."

Some of the high school gang adapted to college in surprising ways. Take Duberg, for example. He pledged Pi Kappa Alpha, got on the swimming team. Started dating a cheerleader. He's still there though, all these years later, tossing the football over the street traffic. Talk about tacky. And for a guy from the Valley, Chris Torres really got into the swing of things. He pledged the Kappa Sigs. I went to one mixer and one football game with him and his fraternity, with a date he arranged for me. That didn't pan out either. His brothers were big on the Confederacy, if you can believe it. There was Chris, a good *vato* from the Valley, yelling and trying to squirt wine into his mouth from a leather pouch and waving the damn Confederate flag. Whistling "Dixie." Now there was a subject for psychology class. Anthropology would even be closer! But beside the pressure to become part of the Confederacy, to become "collegiate," was the course work. Science. Languages. Math. For me the problem was German. And chemistry didn't help. Trigonometry did me in.

Irving and Ben and Phil were pretty much in the same boat. They were just plain guys. From the Valley. River rats like me. We all had big ideas about being pre-engineering, pre-law, pre-med, pre this and that. You know how impressive that seems. Phil wanted to be a pharmacist, and we all kidded him in kind of Mel Blanc, Daffy Duck fashion—"Pphhill the pphharmacistt"—about not being able to reach the "pppilllss" on his store's highest "ssshhhelff." He was a really short guy.

We knew he was sensitive about it. It was all good-natured fun. Even after what happened to him we horsed around and kept kidding him and got him in trouble with the head nurse who found his note in "blood" and really scored him out. We scribbled out the words "Held captive in Room 332" on a prescription pad, signed Phil's name with a big "Rx" beside it, and left it in the elevator. Next visit he told us to lay off—and we did. That one night of Fiesta changed him in lots of ways.

What happened to him was bad. No doubt about that. And I regret it. I'm sorry for it. But we were only half responsible. One way you see it, his shortness, his size was really to blame. And I guess you could trace the causes behind that to him, to his parents, follow it who knows how far back. He was always angry at his "little-guy," "peewee," "shrimp" status. That business about cause and effect came up in more than one class. In some ways I think it's the most basic subject of intellectual inquiry.

Phil was really into the events scheduled for Fiesta weekend. He took charge of getting the tickets for the Saturday night concert and dance. Marty Robbins was the headliner. He was hot then and I liked his songs—"El Paso," "Big Gun," "Flo." Heading down to the West Texas town of El Paso! He had some good ones. I still think of that when I hear the word "border," see old Nick Nolte or Jack Nicholson in border flicks. Hear Christopher Cross flying like the wind, heading for the border of Mexico. But in those days Phil kept raving about Marty Robbins, couldn't stop talking about Marty Robbins. The chance to see Marty Robbins. I knew as soon as the big night came, as soon as I saw Marty, what the big attraction was. He was short. Man, was he short. Even I was surprised—and a bit disappointed, if I'm to be honest. He was about Phil's size. To show you how funny human nature is, Phil wasn't disappointed in the least. Phil was this short man's biggest fan, if I can phrase it that way.

I wasn't as excited about seeing Marty Robbins as I was about the talent show the night before. Sponsored by . . . guess who? Right—the Panhellenic League. I talked Ben into auditioning with me one night over a game of pool. I let him clear the table and then took him over to Okie Joe's for a beer, and pretty soon he gave what everybody called the "Okie Okay."

"Just don't ask me to wear a toga" was his deal breaker.

The place was famous for seductions of all kinds, even "deals" like the one Ben let me think I worked on him. He was worldly-wise and had shown me the ropes more than once, both at Okie Joe's and at Chisholm's. Somehow he always got the prettiest of the pair, so I was justified in my schemes. We knew all the words to "Oklahoma Joe," and Ben was great at double meanings and interpreted the whole thing about swinging back and forward in the saddle, and the pretty good horse with a syncopated gait—all those words—as being all about sex. He did the same thing in his papers for literature class. Went into all kinds of elaborate interpretations. His paper on Kafka's "The Country Doctor" was a classic. The horses. The sick patient. The night. One night in a booth at Chisholm's we picked up a couple of coeds, the slim and the heavy extremes of the "student body," and went cruising around town in Ben's old DeSoto and then to the Cactus Drive-In.

I needn't go into the details of which one sat in the front seat with Ben and how I felt each and every one of the cactus spines painted on the snack bar wall. I went there enough times. But Ben was a fun guy to be around and a strong guy too. Not afraid of anything or anybody. A good-looking guy who could fix a truck tire by hand, just using flatiron tire tools. He worked for a guy named Gonzales at a service station over on Atrisco and Central and carried a long, shiny flatiron tool with a friction tape handle in his car. That night we were glad he did.

The audition was pretty routine. We played and sang a couple of tunes, Everly Brothers style, even did our rendition of "Poor Lonesome Me" and "Blue, Blue Day," which were pretty popular at the time, and thanks to some of Ben's hot licks on his battered Fender Telecaster, got a spot on the show bill. Don Gibson was as plain-looking a guy as ever walked on the stage of the Grand Old Opry; he had two big hits and then pretty much disappeared—never really made it big into country legend, except maybe as a songwriter. Anyway, if I could romanticize old Don Gibson, in all his ordinariness, then I guess it was okay for Phil to identify with Marty Robbins and Ben to emulate Luther Perkins and Scotty Moore. Ben could do Luther's dum, dum, dum, dum "Folsum Prison" bass line in his sleep. As for Scotty's riffs, Ben had all the Elvis "Sun" solos memorized. I was working on the sleepy phrasings of a new kid, Ricky Nelson.

Friday night was the big talent show and Saturday night the big Marty Robbins shindig. We were ready for Fiesta—two nights of it—plus a Saturday afternoon parade down Central in front of Yale Park and then angling off Monte Vista. We had our Western clothes ready. Wore them most of the time anyway. Except this weekend we donned hats. Boots, Western-yoked jackets, Levi's, big-buckled belts. They were uniforms of would-be manliness, I admit it. I even saw old Chris at the dance, and him a bloodline heir to the conquistadores, wearing a cowboy hat. He and his fraternity pals were pretty stewed. Maybe that's why he kind of gave me the cold shoulder. Caballeros, cowboys, big "sombreros" were part of our Western machismo, I guess. Though some Eastern observers must have thought we looked like glorified jackrabbits, maybe even jackasses. That last animal seems more suitable when you think of what happened after the dance and how we regretted it, especially for Phil. For my money, it was the hats that got us into the trouble in the first place. I wasn't looking for a fight. I admit I could have busted some of the geeky Greeks. And did. But I sure didn't bargain for the drunken, wanna-be shit-kicking, pseudo hard-ass hombres we crossed.

I had been to real fiestas out in the Valley—as far north as Bernalillo and south down to Pajarito and Belen. The university came up with the theme of "Fiesta" for its major spring festivity naturally enough. But it's interesting to try and isolate just why a stylized, fake fiesta isn't a real one. What is authenticity anyway? The "real" fiestas I had gone to as a kid with my folks were, after all, twentieth-century adaptations of the even more "real" fiestas in Mexico and Spain reaching back across the centuries. Funny, too, how those institutions, those customs and rituals perpetuate themselves and are adopted and adapted. Folkways. Mores. Assimilation. I was interested in that kind of thing. Maybe that's why I was able to get that good grade from Gribben in sociology. That, and because I had my eye on the girl across from me and wanted to be able to discuss lectures and class notes with her. Phil had his visions of loveliness too. Damn it.

Let me tell you, if you don't already know, an Anglo fiesta on a college campus isn't a Mexican-American, Spanish-American fiesta in the New Mexico and Texas towns along the Rio Grande. Maybe I'm romanticizing that too, but good times are really had by all in those true Valley fiestas—the whole family goes, and cuts the hell loose. You'll see little kids dancing with each other and with their relatives. You'll see young people in love. And old people in love. You'll see people "dancing" in their chairs, in their hearts. And you'll hear that heavy bass line from the guitars and drums, and the melody lines of the fiddles reverberating down through the years, forever in your soul.

Nothing matches those old Mexican melodies, those old dances, the laughter and human sweetness that transport you back to the days when the Spanish and the Mexicans first settled this great Southwest, back to when the mountain men and the trail drivers hit Taos and Santa Fe. "Waugh!" "Eeee ho laaaa!" The real fiestas made you feel alive and young. Made you feel the sadness of life and the joy. How long life lasts and how fleeting it is—and how mysterious and marvelous and tragic.

Maybe that's what the university deans and vice presidents of student services and all the student government leaders who conceived of "Fiesta" and planned it each year, and all the students who whooped it up—maybe that's the kind of thing they had in mind, the old, true fiestas.

But I doubt that most of them had ever really been to a fiesta. They were living in a world of imitations. I had read Plato's "Allegory of the Cave" in fall humanities class, and that's what this Fiesta business seemed like to me. Shadows. With most of the people never really seeing the fire, the source, or knowing about it. And when Phil got stomped, got his ribs broken and his eye kicked out with the sharp toe of that drunk fraternity cowboy's fancy-stitched boot, Plato's little story took on even greater meaning for me. I still think about it. Plato is small potatoes for Phil. He knows the hard, black reality of blindness in his right eye—and the joy of sight in his left one. Maybe he sees that boot speeding toward his face in the stop-time of his nightmares. Sees it in every pill he counts, every prescription he fills, and the hope of every expression of every poor customer who hands him that slip of illegible paper.

He was there in the front row the Friday night of the talent show. Watching Ben and me brave the "Party time!" hoots of the audience one night, and the next night seeing Marty Robbins hit the high notes; those were the last two spectacles he ever saw in full vision. He clapped and whistled and laughed and enjoyed it. You could tell. Other than Phil cheering for us, about all I remember is the empty-headed expression on the Fiesta Queen's face and her lethargic applause as we left the stage. Her escort was some lieutenant commander or admiral in the Naval ROTC!

As far as the dance was concerned, I remember the real pleasure in Phil's face as he listened to Marty Robbins. I remember a couple of dances I had, and I remember the jock with the girl from sociology class. She told me later that he gave her his fraternity pin at Fiesta. Showed it to me there on her soft cashmere sweater. She was all aglow over the big, dumb bastard. I told her about my cuts and bruises and the fight after the dance and what happened to Phil. I told her only in outline, though. Now I could give more attention to raising my grades and forget about the sweetest girl of my dreams and somebody else's reality.

But for weeks, all through the rest of the semester into May's final exams, I relived the fight. Remembered the crowd leaving the dance, Phil's joke about some Greek's drugstore outfit, the squaring off in the parking lot, the darkness and the blows and me ducking a boot, and one of us down and groaning, whimpering. And then the flash of the tire tool and the bang across the hood of their car and Ben vowing to kill the sons of bitches as they ran for cover. And the wetness of the blood pouring through Phil's hand as we loaded him up and sped to the hospital emergency room, just past Okie Joe's. And the grimace of the doctor as he took a first look. And Ben standing in the hall in his torn cowboy shirt. And me, next to him, stunned and angry and remorseful, watching them rush Phil into the operating room, thinking about fun and fiestas and the future, about pain and Phil—and Plato.

TULSA TALK

MAC HAD AN AMAZING STRENGTH IN HIS RIGHT ARM. HE COULD LIFT a trash barrel into the back of his big blue '51 Chevy garbage truck with just that one arm—and the help of his chest and legs. And, as I was to learn, he could do even more marvelous feats along the river with his long-barreled, bolt-action Mossberg shotgun.

When I first knew him he must have been about forty-five or fifty. He had come to the garbage business in a roundabout way. His main specialty was greasing cars. And when he ran the hoist in my father's garage, it was his pride and joy. He swept it with solvent and hosed it down morning and evening. He kept the grease gun shiny with a never-ending supply of red shop rags. He even cleaned the compressor and grease hose as part of his routine.

I guess the idea to start a trash business came from watching Mac clean the shop and haul off the garage and service station trash to the county dump every couple of weeks. There were large converted oil drums positioned at three key points: in the garage, by the side door of the station, and out back. Each Thursday Mac would pick those monsters up like they were toys and load them into the pickup.

So when Dirty Fred put his dump truck and trash route up for sale, my father, ever an entrepreneur, bought him out and put Mac in charge. He did the driving. Loaded the trash. Kept the ledger. He did everything but send out the monthly statements. That was my job as apprentice bookkeeper and budding businessman. To understand my job, and toughen up (for Dad had a sergeant's mentality), I was assigned a week's ride on the garbage route with Mac.

That's where I really came to know him. That's when we became friends and I stopped calling him Bobo the Garbageman with the rest of the help. That's when I started calling him Mac the Knife (I changed it subtly to Mac the Knight) in the tradition of Louis Armstrong, Bobby Darin, and King Arthur.

I never fully understood all the side roads he had been on in his life, his quests, such as they were, or where he was born and what the forces were that led him to become a garbageman. Before I rode the route with him I never really thought much about it. He was black. He had one arm. He was friendly and had a sense of humor. People kidded him and joked with him both to his face and behind his back. He liked to say, "When the boss says, 'Mac, let's you and me do this and do that,' well, sir, that means Mac will do it. I know that for true." And the boss would laugh too.

When some years later, in his "retirement," I drove my newly purchased, yellow '53 Ford convertible to show him one Sunday at his house over on Broadway, he wore an argyle cardigan sweater underneath a gabardine suit jacket. There he was with his worn gray fedora complete with feather in the hatband, tilted at a rakish angle that fell back into place each time he settled it on his head. In his garbage business days he wore an old chauffeur's cap, stained with a ring of dust and sweat.

In retirement his habit still was to remove the hat every minute or two to wipe the perspiration from the leather band, even when he wasn't perspiring. He sat there in front of his house, in the brisk October air, warming his back against the stucco wall, playing checkers, reaching here and there for the smallest of colored cylinders with that one much-used arm.

A kind of South Broadway Satchmo, he kept a clean bandana handkerchief in his breast pocket, and he would reach up with that one still-strong arm, carefully take off his hat and set it cautiously in his lap, reach for the handkerchief and then run it the full circumference of the band. Then he would take the handkerchief back across his breast to its pocket, reach down and under the brim of the hat and pinch the front block in the crown, and raise it slowly to his head. Hat, helmet, or crown, he relied on head wear as long as I knew him.

"This Dobbs was given to me by your father, 'bout five years back, when I quits the trash route and retired. It's a dandy. Long oval, 7 5/8. Fine fit."

It was on that visit, with the memories welling up about our time together as garbagemen, that he told me more things I had never known—about him, about my father, and, by implication, about myself.

I persuaded him to walk over and take a look at my car and he obliged. And I noticed that the scuffed boots of his working days had been replaced by a pair of brogues made to seem all the bigger by the thinness of his ankles and his lightweight white cotton socks.

"You better let me take it up on the grease rack, hear? I can get the grease where it goes, drain and change that oil till the dipstick looks clear as old Vaseline."

He looked under the hood, checked out the belts, and had me show him the air filter. When he was satisfied with the motor and we closed the hood, he looked up and said with a wink, "Don't want to get stall out there up Nine-Mile Hill look'n at the stars and the lights of the city. Gots to stay the route, Frankie."

Just what his life as a young man had been I couldn't imagine. I knew he had been married once but had lived a bachelor for ten or more years. And as we settled back down in front of his house for a game of checkers, I asked him about it.

"Mac, remember when we rode the route you told me you knew my father in Tulsa when you were both younger. Tell me more about how you knew my father in Oklahoma and how you came to work for him out here."

"Don't get me concerted off this game, now. That was a long time back and them times is not pretty ones. No sir. These rumblin's at Washington park and over Robinson's and the civic center, all these city fightings are small. Tulsa had the big riots. Those race riots was where me and your dad mets. That's where I got shot. That's when I lost my arm."

As he maintained his retirement hat and contemplated the best route to checkmate, and traveled old roads talking again about Tulsa, the picture of what had happened to Mac, to my father, and, in its way, to me started to come together. Other memories fell into place.

The dove hunt was the most vivid. One evening we had all loaded into the pickup and driven out to Taylor Ranch and then down to the river bosque for pass shooting. Doves came off the mesas almost as thick as migrating starlings. They darted and dived and swooshed by you. Some of them flew high. And that's where Mac's Mossberg came in. It was a bolt action, if you can believe it, with a thirty-two-inch barrel. Twelve gauge. Full choke. He was decked out in his captain's hat and had a combination game and ammunition pouch slung over his shoulder. And he had the plug removed from his gun so he could load six shells instead of three. Mac the hunter was amazing. He could lift that long goose gun, shoot, and then bring it down to his hip and pull back the bolt, then ram it home and raise the gun for another shot—all in about the time it took the pump-gun hunters in the bunch to fire off two or three shots. And what he aimed at he hit. High shots. Impossible shots that would leave doves, wings extended, spiraling to earth like stalled helicopters.

I remembered that Mac had called his firepower and the barrage of shots fired just at dusk, when the shooting was heaviest, "Tulsa talk." And my father knew what he meant. At the time, he had just said that he and Mac had known each other in Oklahoma.

"Your father was in the same Tulsa riot. Whites after us blacks and blacks after them. Maybe he was one of them that winged me. But I don't imagine so. He didn't want to be in that war any more than I did. We just remember the times. That's why we've been friends out here, out New Mexico. Just one thing bothered me. Him always whistling 'Take Me Back to Tulsa,' while I was the *me* doing *our* work. In some ways we never left the place."

That's why, the more I thought about it driving away from that visit with Mac, showing him my convertible and all, there's still plenty of garbage to haul away. We're all in the garbage business—creating trash and disposing of it. You might even say "garbage" disposal is a noble occupation. One worthy of more souls like Mac. Mac the Knight.

SALVATION

HE LOOKED OUT AT THE CONGREGATION FROM ON HIGH. LAVOLA
was playing the piano softly behind Brother Herschel's vibrato ren-
dering of the familiar, continuing invitation: "Softly and tenderly,
Jesus is calling, calling, / oh sinner, come home. / Come home, /
Come home. Ye who are weary, come home."

Lavola breathed hard, pushing her ample chest out and back, up
and down, in rhythm with the hymn. The sanctuary was humid and
warm, and it made breathing even more difficult for her.

He saw her as she had been with him earlier, before the main
worship service, which had just ended, white and pliant and breathing hard. Now the curtains had been pulled and the baptistry water
sloshed around his waders and against the waist-high glass panel that
allowed the faithful to see the spectacle of the baptism, the dunking
of the believer, Lavola's husband, Thestal—a drama scheduled in
the bulletin to take place "immediately following the service."

Last week, in preparation for this time, the minister had thrown
the boots in the back of his 1954 Chevrolet 3100 series panel truck
and taken them down to Brother Haskill's Shamrock station, and had
Glen put on two new hot patches. Haskill had assured him he would
supervise Glen personally.

What the preacher felt now was either the result of a new leak or
a careless job done on one of the old holes, probably by old man
Marshall rather than Glen. The buffing, or the glue, or the targeting
of the patches hadn't been right. Already the preacher's left foot and

ankle were wet. "Good thing Haskill wasn't in the prophylactic business!" the preacher joked to himself.

He could feel the water oozing in, and, like a fly-fisherman aiming for a backswirl, he cast another long look at Lavola, seated there at the faded, fruitwood piano, positioned off to the right side of the pulpit. He thought of their time together hours earlier in his study. Lavola looked up, and her eyes rose to his glance with an ambivalent expression of joy and fear.

Her face was still flushed and she looked disheveled, with her familiar eight-karat-gold heart locket not really centered in the soft spot where it usually rested, low on her cotton-soft, reddened, now slightly bruising throat. A curl of her dark, sweaty-sweet hair stood out, untamed, over her left temple, aggravating her ear, which still tingled from his love bites upon it. The reverend took his own deep breath.

He hadn't plotted it at all, he told himself, reviewing their brief, recent history. She surely hadn't deliberately "seduced" him. There was no premeditation or evil forethought, at least not consciously, in their union, their coming together that way. He didn't even think, at the time, to command Satan behind him, as he had done in past opportunities of the kind. What happened just happened. It was a need not met, apparently, in their respective marriages.

He had opened the water pipes to fill up the baptistry and had returned down the carpeted back stairs and around the corner into the pastor's study—his own sanctuary, as the congregation respectfully referred to it. He was readying his worn-out rubber boots and the text of what he must say as part of the few passages of fixed and formal liturgy in the hymnal for the performance of this sacred church event, the holy rite and sacrament of baptism.

He would preach his sermon, then exit and prepare himself and Thestal, and then, in turn, they would wade down into the baptistry. Pastor Ron was a fisherman of women—and men. Mostly he would pray, recall his own river-rushing immersion as a boy in Amarillo, Texas, invoke the Holy Trinity . . . and improvise as the words came to him and the Spirit of the Lord moved him.

He remembered Lavola entering the study quite early that morning to say hello and double-check the bulletin for the songs she was to play and Brother Herschel was to sing.

"Was there . . . anything . . . you wanted changed, Reverend?" Her voice was happy and believing and enticing, and in its tendency to pause and catch between certain words, it drew him into curious anticipation of what she might say next. He remembered somehow, momentarily, associating that voice with Patsy Cline—sultry, provocative, in need.

Standing there talking to him in his white T-shirt on such a fresh spring morning in her Sunday-simple best dress, Lavola was clearly no Nashville star, but still and all, she was a much prettier woman than she had appeared at first look, those few short weeks ago when he accepted the call to preach and lead the congregation at this small Valley church, Bethlehem Baptist. Even at choir practice and on past Sundays he had never really noticed her body, its conformations, the well-defined, inviting contours beneath her clothes.

She wore no makeup and tried to keep her lustrous black hair uncurled and rolled high on her head. Her skin was unblemished and creamed smooth, with none of the dry porousness of his wife's, of Mildred's, Texas tumbleweed, weather-hardened complexion.

This Sabbath day Lavola had greeted him with the proper blend of respect and friendliness, calling him Brother Ron, as instructed at their first introduction. In readying for the baptismal service he asked her to pray with him. After all, Thestal was her husband, and she had come with him to the little planning and preparation meeting last Wednesday night after choir practice and prayer meeting.

This day he talked to her of the glories of spring and Sunday morning and the risen Lord. He touched her hand, held it tighter. He caressed her arm and then stroked her hair, softly and tenderly removing the clasp and letting it cascade around her neck and shoulders. He kissed her neck and ears, then lightly touched both lobes with his lips.

Next thing he knew, they were embracing and she was out of her dress and slip. Her bra was off and her undergarments kicked away. And she was straddling him, wet and easy, on his desk, his pants hanging from his shoes, held only by the overlapping tongues and protruding laces. Lavola was spellbound, automatic in acquiescing to Brother Ron's caresses, somehow envisioning herself, in that act, submitting to Thestal, to all men, to the Lord! But this was ecstasy, a conversion, a resurrection of her body and her rushing blood, and she kept saying, "It's good, Ron, it's good, Lord, it's good. God. God." And she pushed him down on the desktop, knocking over his basket of papers and letters. She was wild and frantic upon him, bringing him to pleasures of aggression which Mildred, which Lavola herself, had never shown.

The pastor's lilac cologne and well-barbered freshness, just the simple appeal of his clean hands and fingernails, made his touch on her and in her all the more welcome and needed. She squirmed and sighed and kissed him repeatedly on the forehead, the neck, the chest, and then time and again hard and long on the mouth.

The thought of plum blossoms, plum blossoms in the orchards he had known as a child in Texas, intruded strangely on his consciousness. The sweet smell of her skin—and her breasts . . . plumlike, eager and responsive to his reaching, white and beautifully plum-tipped, plump and firm and resilient to his touch . . . the nipples dark and large and extended . . . and he bit them too with his lips, and lightly with his teeth—and she was warm and smooth and wet, a wetness that mixed with his, engulfing him, baptizing him in the sin and guilt and glory of their flesh, the violation of God's commandment against such a betrayal of his vows to his wife, words said in a small Texas church where he was saved and called to the service of the Lord, where he was married to his wife—good, obedient, caring Mildred, mother of his four children, sitting there where she always sat wherever he preached, here for nearly a full month of Sundays now, Sunday after Sunday after Sunday, second row center, with Peggy, Ruth, Beaumont, and little Matthew.

The first church, in Texhoma, was not unlike this church in New Mexico, this place where there were two kinds of believers, Roman Catholic and Southern Baptist; this place called Bethlehem Baptist in Bernalillo, the church he was struggling to revive as a mission church of the big First Baptist Church farther down the valley in Albuquerque; the church where earlier that very Sunday, in his study, for heaven's sake, he had fucked and been fucked in return, giving a new meaning (he had to smile in thinking it), to the Christian "principles of reciprocity" that had been stressed so much in seminary.

He felt it again—this bothersome, mischievous ambivalence, wanting to smile at his shame and his sin—throughout the service and the sermon on Pentecost and the founding of the church. And even now he could still feel Lavola's soft and tender wetness lingering there like the song, like her song, lingering with him even to her plum-blossom breasts and her musky odor mixing with the lilac aroma of his shaving lotion, still there lapping like the baptistry waters against his legs and the thick glass in front, longing to burst forth and escape, surrounding him, merging with his own sticky, drenched legs.

And he stiffened again and swooned to the rhythm and music of her sex and the sounds and motions of her hands on the upright piano, stroking it "softly and tenderly," calling to sinners like him, Pastor Ron Decker, a sinner now more than ever in need of salvation and spiritual cleansing, in need of washing in the blood, a sinner in need of love and . . . Lavola, a sinner who now reached up—thinking of plum blossoms again and of Lavola's lovely, heavy, pendulous breasts—reached up to Lavola's own husband, Brother Thestal Briscoe, a convert of a different sort, and led him by the hand down the slick steps into the tank, with his own bellowing and bespoiled yet believing anthem of rebirth: "Enter the kingdom of the Lord, Brother Briscoe. Blessed be His name. All praise be His. Hallelujah, brothers and sisters, hosanna on high. Christ has risen and is moving us today."

Thestal stepped cautiously, one large, bare foot at a time, down the crude, challenging, slippery metal steps into the water and stood, shivering, in front of the preacher. Then he glanced sheepishly, his chin quivering, over at his wife. Lavola kept her eyes on the pages of the green-covered hymnal and tried hard to improve the technique of her right hand while she worked the foot pedals in a flourish of worry and pleasure.

She could feel perspiration mixing with that special wetness coming again, yet again, between her legs, and with each new pressure on the sustaining pedals she warmed again to the hard and

hot entry of the preacher inside her and the rhythms she had improvised, almost in Edenic ecstasy. Only distantly she heard Brother
Ron whisper, "Bless you, Thestal. Come, Child of God into His
name. Fear not. Turn around now, my brother, and face the congregation, the brotherhood of baptized believers."

Standing there in the water, in his white shirt, buttoned at the top
and at the sleeves, and in his threadbare, but just washed and ironed,
work jeans (jeans that, ordinarily, he wore for Saturday yard work at
home and just yesterday for helping the church building and grounds
committee in their raking and watering, painting and plastering
service for the Lord), Thestal turned and stood square-shouldered
beside the preacher. Trusting. Accepting. Innocent of what had
happened between Pastor Ron and Lavola—and what was yet to
happen.

The man was a full head taller than Brother Ron, and his shoulders seemed to hold his white shirt up and away from his neck like a
wooden clothes hanger. Without his glasses he couldn't really see the
features of the faces that looked up at his. Couldn't really see Lavola
when, squinting, he searched for her.

His was a litheness come from hard work at the lumber and
hardware store where he ran the saws and stocked the lumber and
drywall and bags of cement and plaster and filled the nail bins. He
knew about such things, could rip through a two-by-eight at just the
right places, could turn the small forklift on a dime, knew about
building supplies and construction; in fact, he had built his and
Lavola's and their young son's, Billy's, small frame stucco home on
Beverly Road, not far from Pastor Ron's parsonage, provided by the
church. Thestal had helped too, in filling the lumber and lath order
and in manning the renovation crew led by Haskill and the church
deacons to ready things for Brother Ron and Mildred's moving
in. Thestal was a good soul, everyone could testify to that—even
Lavola.

Now, at this moment, Mrs. Ritchie looked out from behind
Mildred's shoulder and noticed Thestal's white skin around his ears
and temples, evidence of time in the sun and yesterday afternoon's
fresh haircut, and chanted loudly, "Glory to God, Thestal! Glory to
God on high!"

Thestal recognized her voice. Lavola ceased playing "I Am Weak But Thou Art Strong" but kept her head bowed, self-consciously dramatizing the reverence and solemnity of the moment. Thinking of her own baptisms, past and recent, holy and profane wetness, blessed wetness and the wetness of perspiration—and the other wetness, she couldn't help it, now saturating her. She was among the church believers, among the baptized. Salvation!

Brother Bob Fowlers had baptized her. And she had told Thestal and Billy about it more than once. Thestal's acceptance of the Lord had come from Pastor Fowlers too, from Brother Bob's last sermon before he left Bethlehem for a larger church in Enid. The months waiting for Brother Ron to come to Bethlehem and consummate Thestal's conversion had been hard to bear for them both and for the congregation sitting through the seemingly endless roster of visiting preachers, all hoping for the call. Now she realized she had been baptized too by Pastor Ron. Baptized into another kind of awareness. Damnation!

"We are gathered here today, good brethren, to baptize our friend and fellow believer in Christ, Thestal W. Briscoe. He has answered the call, answered Christ's knocking at the door of his heart, and he has let Him in as we all have and as we must again when we rededicate, through this action, our hearts to Him. Now Thestal will share with us the comfort of knowing salvation, the peace that comes from accepting God's grace and love in reaching out to us, his wayward flock. Christ, the Good Shepherd, will not rest when one, even one, single solitary sheep is lost. He will venture forth and find us and embrace us and bring us home, saved. 'For God so loved the world that He gave His only begotten Son, that whosoever believeth in Him shall not perish but have life everlasting.' Remember the Scripture, sinner. Remember the promise of redemption. Good works will not save you. There is only one heavenly path, and that is by believing in Him and renouncing the once glorified and accepted but finally fallen and cast-out Lucifer. Only by confessing publicly your belief in Christ the Lord will salvation be yours in the eternal fight between good and evil, the SAVED and the LOST, the sheep and the goats. Only through baptism, sinner, will you be born again and enter the gates of heaven. Now Brother Thestal comes home. Let us hear him renounce his sins and with him renounce our own again."

"I confess. I am a sinner. I accept Christ as Savior. I believe in God and in Jesus his only Son, who died for my sins."

"Holy! Holy! Holy!" cried out from the front pew the council president and the church's most esteemed deacon, Mr. Terrell.

"Praise be his name" came the deep, resonating shout of Brother Herschel from his place behind the altar and beneath the baptistry. "Let us gather by the river, the beautiful, beautiful river."

Then Brother Ron placed his right hand on Thestal's trusting back and his left hand over Thestal's nose and mouth and lowered him into the water, stumbling and for a time losing his balance from the height and size of the man.

"I baptize you in the name of the Father," said the preacher in a now strained and strident voice. Thestal's buoyancy was strong, and he was hard to hold under the magic, wavy waters.

And then he raised Thestal up and out, out of the water, dripping, spewing, his long arms flailing and his hard hands slapping and feeling for equilibrium again, like a large brown trout pulled out of the Rio Chama, a lunker of sublime size and fight hitting the surface of the water with its tail, riled, angry at the hooked fly pulling at its mouth, miffed, like the leviathan at the obstruction of Noah. The pastor's muscles ached and he feared Thestal's strength and knew he wanted nothing of this simple, naive man's real wrath.

"I baptize you in the name of the Son," came the preacher's echoing burst of words.

The attention of the congregation—especially that of the baptized believers—was complete and intense. They felt again the waters of their own immersion and, mystically, knew again their own bursting-forth out of the fluids, the blood and the salt, of birth. Lavola gasped more rapidly, more empathetically, for breath and felt her heart beat behind the constrictions of her too-hastily-snapped brassiere. Mildred blew her nose and dabbed her eyes and reached over to try and subdue Beaumont in his attempts to stab his brother, Matt, with his black rubber dagger, which he had deviously smuggled out of the house and brought to church.

Deacon Terrell and Mrs. Ritchie were moaning and rocking back and forth in their best-view pews. Brother Rudy Sandford was already on his feet with his arms raised heavenward, reciting his own medley of Scripture: " 'Speak unto all the congregation of the children of Israel, and say unto them, Ye shall be holy: for I the Lord your God am Holy.' Leviticus, chapter nineteen, verse two." He had read the Bible through five times, he said. His repertoire of memorized verses gave credence to his boast.

Brother Herschel had turned to face the baptistry and was on one knee, praying and shuttling his maroon-and-white polka-dotted handkerchief back and forth from his forehead to his suit coat—forehead to pocket, forehead to pocket, in sympathy with the back and forth swaying of the congregation, and allowing his oversized ID bracelet and pinkie ring to arc golden against the austerity of the sanctuary paneling and the curtains of the baptistry.

Little William Briscoe was seated quietly by an open north window, preoccupied with the spring chirpings and skitterings of sparrows in a nearby tree and trying to give his own simplified, tabulated accounting of them—like his Sunday School teacher, Mrs. Frazer, in the lesson of the day, said Christ could of both the flying and the fallen. Billy envied the sparrows in their jumping and flying and chirping outside in the cool air. His arms and legs ached and he felt dizzy and very hot. His head ached too, and he had a hard time keeping it from swaying from one shoulder to the next. The whole congregation ebbed and flowed in their own various, personalized, hysterical swaying, little tidal spasms and convolutions of faith, as if some magnetic moon were pulling them into the motions and motives of the waters of the baptistry.

"I baptize you in the name of the Holy Ghost," came the preacher's finale, completing the Trinity, and down went Thestal into the waters of the tank again, and the congregation held its collective breath with him and tried with him to see through the murky waters past the pastor's wading boots, past the containing glass, into eternity and the destination of their individual souls as true but backsliding believers, as among the baptized, as men and women and children born to live, born to death, born to sin and salvation, mortality and life everlasting.

Then, amid the prophecies and revelations—glimpsed or not seen—in their own lives, in their own inquisitions of faith, by all the people there, Thestal somehow pulled Brother Ron under the water with him, his long arms wrapping around him almost as if the biblical leviathan from the deep had pulled him under. Such was the wages of sin, the result not of Thestal's wrath but of God and the risen Lord and the Scriptures, which taught one to know better, to resist the temptations of the flesh and the world.

"Look, Daddy's gone under too," yelled Peggy, and she stood up, frightened, and pointed toward the thrashing figures seen beneath the baptistry waters. Beaumont and Matthew wrestled each other to their feet to gawk. Billy tried to stabilize his wavering head and focus on the commotion, on the words and movements. He could make out his father's white shirt under the water, churning and churning like his mother's loads of wash, which hypnotized him, bouncing and spinning behind the little round glass doors, down at Mr. Mabrey's All-Points Laundromat.

"Oh, Lord, Lord, help them, Brother Herschel," came Mrs. Ritchie's scratchy scream. "Save them, somebody, Thestal'll, . . . they'll drown."

But just as Brother Herschel rose from his kneeling, the preacher and Thestal shot high and fast out of the water together. And Thestal was up and standing and witnessing as in the days of Babel.

"Lord, I'm saved. Poor sinner saved and baptized at last," he repeated through a waterlogged but beaming smile. And nonsensical syllables and sounds spewed forth in an unrecognizable language. Speaking in tongues. He was, indeed, speaking in tongues. The preacher stood shocked, frightened and gasping for air. Once before at a tent revival meeting in Pampa he had witnessed such extravagant expression of faith. And then, after glancing furtively at Lavola, he too raised both his arms to heaven, saying loudly, "Thy will be done, Thy will be done!"

And Lavola, stunned beyond guilt, rallied, sat back on the piano bench and struck hard at the keyboard of the spinet, ringing out the chords and melody of the introductory refrain, while Brother Herschel cried out rapidly, "Hymn number 267, number 267" and on the wide wave of the downbeat began to measure out the tempo with the generous, exaggerated arcs of his glittering right hand, began to do what he was reborn to do some five years back during Brother Winifred Green's crusade for Christ: lead the singing! His voice boomed over the excited congregation, "Let me hear it; God's glory in song!"

While Brother Ron listened to Thestal stammer and watched him walk with bare, sure feet back up the stairs of the baptistry, resurrected, dramatically, in a robe of dripping water and incomprehensible words, the congregation sang forth in jubilation their memories, their belief, and their expectation, "When the roll is called up yonder,/When the roll is called up yonder, / When the roll is called up yonder, / When the roll is called up yonder, I'll be there."

Lavola added an extra flourish of arpeggios at the end of each stanza, relieved as much by Brother Ron's escape as by her husband's palavering salvation, for in those eternal moments when they were both under the water she had feared the vengeance of the Lord as much as his saving grace. Now Thestal was hooked on religious conversion, a zealot devoted to other worlds. He was forgiven—and could surely forgive should he ever find out.

She played one more hymn of her own choosing and thanksgiving, "Amazing Grace," while the congregation filed out of the sanctuary and onto the walkways and grounds in front of the church. Closing her hymnal and holding it for an extra few minutes against her chest, she thought of the confusing knot of the two men under the water, and her transgression early that morning with the pastor, thought of his lilac-loving ways and his hands on her body, touching her there, and all over, and her own perspiration and fluid-drenched neck and legs, and she looked out at the empty pews and saw her son, Billy, still seated at the end of the pew by the window. His head lay limp against the hard back of the wooden bench and he was pale, as white as the clouds outside the open window that framed him.

She dropped the hymnal with a dead thud and ran toward him, crying, "Thestal, Thestal, my God, Billy's not right. Here, in the church, in the church! Somebody, please somebody come quick and help."

Thestal came running, with Pastor Ron, from the side choir door at the front of the church. They had changed clothes, back into

Sunday suits, and their hair was still wet and slicked back, glistening. The preacher's tie hung long and untied beneath his shirt collar.
The three of them reached Billy at the same time, but it was Lavola
who sat down beside him and cradled his head, saying, "He's
burning up with fever. He said he had a stomachache on the way to
Sunday school, but I thought he was just dreading going. He's sick,
very sick."

Thestal hunkered down and spoke to the boy, "Son, wake up.
What's wrong? Are you sick? You've got a fever. Where does it
hurt?"

Billy partially opened his eyes and whined, "My arms and legs
ache. It's worse than growing pains . . . worse."

"Doc Hall . . . we've got to get him to Doc Hall right now!"
Lavola cried out with urgency.

"Now, Lavola, he'll be okay," replied the preacher and placed
his hand tenderly on her shoulder. "Calm down. Don't overreact.
Let's take him home first, make him comfortable with blankets in the
back of my Chevy, and call Doc Hall out to your house. We can carry
Billy out to the truck. Bring the pew cushion."

Thestal had the boy picked up and in his arms carrying him down
the aisle and toward the church door before Lavola could reply. She
ran hastily back to the piano for her purse and then followed the
procession of preacher, father, and son past the milling crowd and to
the dented and rusting panel truck, the family truck, which Pastor
Ron drove on his errands and visitations and which was always down
at Haskill's being worked on. Mildred and the kids were standing by
the truck, which looked something like an ambulance or emergency
vehicle anyway, waiting for Ron as he hurriedly opened the two back
doors wide and climbed in to make a place for Billy.

"What's the matter, Ron? What's wrong with him? Is it the
Briscoe boy?" inquired Mildred in a concerned but lethargic tone.
"Where are you taking him?"

"Mildred, Billy's real sick. You and the kids get a ride home with
Brother Herschel or someone. I'm taking Billy and his family home
so they can get the boy in bed and call Doc Hall."

"I want to come too!" insisted Beaumont, his rubber knife
tucked ostentatiously into his belt.

"Me too. Me too," chimed in the other Decker children.

But Thestal was handing Billy to Ron at the back of the truck and Lavola was climbing in beside him. The preacher gave the pew cushion one last tug and covered Billy with an old quilt that he kept on hand, and then stepped over his tackle box and fishing pole and some loose tools, into the driver's seat. Thestal closed the back doors tightly, peeked once through the rear windows, and ran to the passenger side and jumped in. Pastor Ron turned on the ignition, pumped the accelerator four or five times, slammed the floor shift into reverse, and backed onto the road.

Mildred shaded her eyes with her hand and watched as the Chevy pulled away in a cloud of street dust and black exhaust smoke. Her tongue felt a piece of sand on her front teeth. And she distantly felt Beaumont stabbing her in the right hip and then in the side with his rubber knife, while the girls ran off into the curious congregation, looking for a ride.

Pastor Ron stuck his arm out the window to signal for a left turn into the station, waited for one car to pass, then a second, saw it was clear and gunned it for a quick trajectory into the driveway and a fast-braking, metal-scraping halt at the "regular" pump where he always stopped. There were high cumulus clouds to the south and east but the sun glared down on the faded, forest-green hood of the truck, reflecting off the white and kelly green of the large Shamrock pole sign. He reached back behind the seat and grabbed his rubber wading boots, limp and cool to his touch, not, he thought, like Billy Briscoe, yesterday. Then the preacher pulled twice on the door handle and stepped down out of the cab, partially turning to slam the door. He had his weekday suit on, a brown-and-gray twill worn bare around the cuffs and at the elbows and knees. Mildred always kept his shirts ironed and fresh, and the blue one he wore today on his Monday rounds was accented by a turquoise-and-coral bolo tie, one that Mildred gave him when they were first married, before the kids started coming. He leaned down to brush a shoe smudge off his pant leg and raised up just in time to be greeted by Haskill and the station front men, Glen and old man Marshall.

"Fill her up today, Brother Ron, and check under the hood?"

Glen was still carrying part of his lunchtime sandwich, and the preacher glimpsed the mix of mustard, white bread, and bologna in his mouth.

"Yes, Glen, thank you. I'm sure she needs oil. And check the right front tire too, she's pulling like a one-arm bandit at the Elks Club this morning."

Haskill extended his hands, saying, "What's with the boots again, preacher? All that ruckus under the water yesterday cause 'em to spring another leak? I'll patch the patches; patch 'em till we run out of patches and glue. All part of my contribution to the church and the Lord. Hand 'em over."

"I think Glen or Marshall there missed a hole or two. Check the left one at the seam. I think that's where it's leaking. And the right one has a small hole higher up, midway." Old man Marshall let fly a spit of tobacco and resumed his slow-motioned silence.

Haskill took the boots. He loved operating his station and talking to his customers and dressed and acted the part, complete with a spiffy green Shamrock windbreaker and a black bow tie, which he always bragged about hand-tying—no dinky clip-ons for him. He had an eye for politics and was contemplating a run for county commissioner if the Democratic primary didn't line up too many candidates. People at the church said they would support him, pass out leaflets and campaign for him.

"How's the Briscoe boy?" Haskill asked. "He get scared at his father's going under for the third time, in flesh and spirit, and not coming up on schedule? Old Thestal just about took you down under with him, didn't he, preacher?"

"I'm going over to see the boy later this afternoon. His mother wanted me to say a special prayer. Doc Hall came over after Lavola and Thestal got him into bed. Swabbed his throat and gave him some aspirin for the aches. Said to give him plenty of water and to watch him for a few days. The kid says it hurts to move his legs and arms."

Glen appeared from under the hood with dipstick and rag in hand: "Say, preacher, you're two quarts low again. Still want the bulk oil?"

"Sure, Glen, sure," said Haskill. "Whatever this buggy needs and charge it to the church account. Just don't put that oil in the radiator. Charity always begins at work, I always say—at least for Brother Ron here. Come on inside and have a Coke and some peanuts. Candy bars aplenty in the machine."

Marshall moved for the air hose, and Glen followed his boss and the preacher inside the station and levered out two quarts of cheap bulk oil and walked back to the pastor's insatiable vehicle. While the oil drained into the motor, he filled the radiator with water, and went on to help the old man wash the windshield and the two rear windows. Glen secured the gas cap and closed the rickety hood and had the charge ticket already written by the time Pastor Ron came out of the station again, hoisting his suit pants and checking their zipper.

"The pause that refreshes, Glen," he said as he reached the truck and took his copy of the charge ticket. "Better even than a long spurt of tobacco, right, old man?" but Marshall had turned and was already on his way back to his stool inside. The preacher sat down behind the wheel again while Glen gave the windshield another couple of swipes and rubbed off a drop of oil on the fender. Then, over the roar of the truck motor Pastor Ron leaned out and yelled to Haskill, "See you in church," gave an okay hand sign to Glen, saw an opening in the traffic, and headed off toward town and his afternoon of employments and visitations. The morning meant a stop at the Osteopathic Physicians and Surgeons Hospital (Mrs. Sandford, Rudy's mother, was there with stomach ailments). He read Scripture with her and talked small talk and church news. Now, in the afternoon, he was on his way to officiate at Grandpa Ritchie's funeral, first at Crownfield's Mortuary and then on out to the Garden Grove Cemetery. Finally (before suppertime, he hoped), to the Briscoes' house and prayers for Billy. The thought of seeing Lavola got him through the morning and, he hoped, would get him through the funeral.

The first drop of rain splattered on the thin paper, spreading quickly up and down and out to the gilded edges. Brother Ron closed his deluxe edition, red-letter, gilt-edged, Nelson Bible, another gift from Mildred, quoted the rest of the verse, Psalm 23, from memory, bowed his head and uttered a hastened, prayerful good-bye to the old man.

Grandpa Ritchie was the first baptized member of Bethlehem and had lived a long life, and an active one right up to the end at eighty-seven. Now his body was being lowered for another kind of resurrection one day. His spirit as a believer was no doubt already winging heavenward. His wife, now crying in the rain beside the grave, had not missed a church service in all the years of the mission's existence and knew the rolls of all the living and the dead. She was the one designated by the church to issue the call to Brother Ron.

He stared at the rivulets of water now trickling into the grave as the casket began its descent and thought of Thestal Briscoe's untoward baptism and about Lavola and the prayers he promised to say for Billy. Lavola's life and loveliness, their newly found passionate desire for each other's bodies, took on a new intensity against the memory flashes of Mrs. Sandford's frail, brittle, and dried-out form on her hospital bed, the sounds of the lowering casket, and the hard, rain-slick tombstones that dotted the periphery of his vision. The gloom and finality of what he saw eroded what he preached, what he accepted by faith, so that each clod of fresh dirt that the water swept over the edge increased his longing for Lavola.

Maybe, just maybe, there would be time at her house, out of Billy's way, and before Thestal came home from work at the lumberyard. The others were now running for their cars, and he too turned quickly, shoving his Bible under his coat and turning up the collar as he checked himself and took a few long strides over to Mrs. Ritchie to comfort her and the family one last time.

By the time he made it to the truck his coat was soaked—and his shirt, from the collar all the way down to the front pocket. Forget the small trouser smudges of the morning. His resoled shoes were caked with mud, covering the wing-tipped toes, and the splatters from hitting the last large puddle went as high as his knees.

"Should have kept my boots with me, damn it!" It was an outburst made as much in vanity as in anger. "Can't track it in Lavola's house."

But his spirits could not be subdued, and once off the gravel road and back on Central he started to hum with the syncopated rhythm of the one wiper that worked, streaking and squeaking over the windshield. "I come to the garden alone, / While the dew is still on the roses, / . . . . And He walks with me, and He talks with me, / And

He tells me I am His own." It was one of old man Ritchie's final requests, and Brother Herschel sang it up swell at the mortuary service. Now, Pastor Ron's involuntarily choosing to sing that song on the way to see Lavola struck him as immensely funny and he laughed to himself and reached to turn on the knobless radio. Julie London . . . "Now you say you love me. / Well just to prove you do, why don't you cry me a river, cry me a river, / I cried a river over you." The song stirred him forward with an even heavier foot on the gas pedal, and he envisioned Lavola's body, her breasts, and the tautness of her arms—and moist . . .

He made it by the Santa Fe shops just as the 3:00 P.M. whistle drowned out the siren song on the radio. By 3:10 he whirred past his own house, a risk worth taking since that was the shortest route, and, veering around a small pond of standing rain runoff, turned into the Briscoe driveway. He meant to ask Haskill to fix the turn signal on the left fender—probably just a burned-out bulb. And only the rain-sogged air kept the Chevy's radiator from overheating in the rush of reaching Lavola—and Billy. The rain had let up, and he saw Lavola peering through the rain-glazed living room window. She motioned him to the back porch. The house was recently stuccoed, darkened by the plaster-soaking rain, and the lawn was greening from the first turnings of showers like this one and Thestal's weekly irrigating from the waters of his own well and pump. It was a well-kept house, one that Thestal obviously took pride in as its builder and its caretaker.

The preacher darted out of the truck, across the gravel driveway and inside the screened-in back porch. Lavola held the screen door open for him, seeing that his suit coat was soaked and his trousers mud-spattered.

"Oh, Pastor Ron, take off that coat and those muddy shoes. And come in, come in. I told Billy you wouldn't forget to come by and say a prayer for him. He's in the living room on the couch." The preacher laughed and did as instructed. "Maybe I can pray better in my stocking feet. The Lord never wore wing tips doing His work."

He followed Lavola through the small kitchen and dining room and into the living room. The couch was arranged in front of the large window that faced out to the west and Beverly Road. Billy's head was propped up on the arm of the couch with two cleanly cased bedroom pillows, and a sunbeam coursed its way across his face, giving him a heavenly, surreal appearance, like a figure out of a painting by one of the masters. He was glaring at the minute particles of lint and dust suspended airily in the beam. He didn't acknowledge the preacher at first.

"Well, Billy, my boy, you look a little less peaked than you did yesterday. Gave us a start there for a while. Guess the ride in the pastor's emergency truck shook you back on the road to recovery. Do you feel better? The Lord works in mysterious ways and although it's hard for us to always see the reasons, we must accept them."

"It hurts to walk. My legs and arms ache."

"His fever's down. But he had to roll off his bed onto my back for me to carry him in here and fixed up on the couch for your visit. He's a little big to be riding piggyback, don't you think, Pastor Ron? Can you picture me crawling in here on my hands and knees with Billy on my back? What a mother won't do for her children. But he does ache, and he isn't the kind to play possum with us. When Thestal gets home from work, he'll just swoop him up and carry him back to bed."

"Oh, I know that, Lavola. Remember, I have Beaumont to gauge these things by. Let's get right to the prayer, what do you say? Doc Hall has his ways and the Lord has His own. You sit on the edge of the couch with Billy, and I'll scoot up a dining room chair."

The preacher walked back into the dining room and picked up a chair. Lavola couldn't help smiling at the sight of him walking in his socks and couldn't resist imagining him naked and . . . But she was stirred back into the purpose of the moment soon enough when he placed the chair beside her and the boy lying on the couch and still staring at the sunbeam radiating across his field of vision.

"Let us join hands in the name of the Lord," he said and reached for Lavola's and Billy's hands while she softly secured Billy's other hand. The preacher gently rubbed the back of Lavola's hand with his thumb. Billy winced from the agitation to his hands and arms and Pastor Ron, with a whispered request for bowed heads, began his prayer for healing:

"Lead us in Thy truth. Allow us to accept Thy will, full knowing that all things work to the best for those who love and have faith in the Lord. We ask that this boy come to a full and fast recovery. If the faith of a grain of mustard seed can move a mountain, our faith will restore Billy to wholeness. Heal this boy, we pray. Let him walk painlessly in the path of the Lord. Let him climb up, up that sunshine mountain. In the name of the Lord Who taught us to pray we ask . . . Thy will be done. Amen."

Loosening Billy's hand and raising his head, Pastor Ron opened his eyes into Lavola's gaze, for she had been looking at him during the prayer and returning the caresses of his thumb and fingers with her own. She quickly responded, "He'll get well now. Look, his eyes are closed and he's resting." Together, they let go of Billy's hands and softly stood up and backed away from the couch.

Still holding the preacher's hand and facing him, Lavola whispered, "Doc Hall wants to call in a specialist down at Lovelace Clinic. He thinks it may be some form of polio or some other paralysis. I'm so worried and so is Thestal. But all I can think about is you. My life is suddenly a mess. I think the Lord is punishing me for my transgression. Can you pray for me, too?

His kiss curtailed her words and there in her own living room in front of her ill, sleeping son he reached down and started to slide her dress up her tender white legs. When he reached the soft, moist mound of his desire, she broke loose and pulled him out of the living room and back through the dining room and kitchen and onto the back porch. There in the corner of the porch, on the cushioned, oversized, metal-tracked, swing-sofa they satisfied their animal passions—to a cacophony of squeaking noise and the swaying, arrhythmic motion of the clanging, jerking antique porch swing. The braying and squawking of all the Brementown musicians was no match for the wildness of sibilant sighs, guttural grunts, and clanging iron that rose to the kitchen window which looked out on the porch and behind which echoed the horrified, hand-muffled groans of little Billy Briscoe, come to tell the two wondrous, wriggling figures known to him as mother and Pastor Ron—now lost to him and each other—that the prayer had worked and he could walk.

When Thestal said the blessing for what turned out to be their last supper, he thanked the Lord for Billy's recovery and for Lavola and

their home and for his job at the hardware and lumber store. Somewhere between a request for another piece of round steak and the
green beans and gibberish about sunbeams and the sunshine mountain, Thestal put down his fork and listened to Billy with new
attention.

"Pastor Ron wrestled with Mom on the porch like he did with
you in the water Sunday morning at church."

Thestal's first response was a laugh. "Your fever got the best of
you, son."

Then came a few more questions directed to Billy—and to
Lavola. A denial was followed by Lavola's admission that what Billy
said was true.

"It happened, Thestal. We did it at the church too. I can't deny it.
We can't resist the temptation. I confess. I'll . . . pray for the Lord's
forgiveness—and yours. But the pull between the pastor . . . and
me is stronger than forgiveness and love . . . than words or Scripture
or . . . whatever. It's an amazing, transforming power, like the
power of salvation itself. Forgive me if you can. I'm sorry for you
that it happened this way, Thestal. I'm sorry, Billy—if you can
understand any of this."

Thestal's eyes watered and then fixed themselves in a straight-
ahead stare, fixed and inward-looking, in a glazed-over gaze through
his tear-smeared, salt-stained glasses. He rose from the table, walked
through the dining room into the bedroom, and reached high into the
closet, where his hand found its way to the gun he kept there—a .32
Colt automatic with a full clip of eight small, streamlined copper-
cased and lead-tipped bullets. He rammed one into the chamber and
was out of the house, backing out of the driveway in the hardware
store's red Ranchero Ford, and headed for Pastor Ron's house by the
time Lavola got through on the phone to the parsonage. Peggy
answered, and yelled for Mildred over the commotion of trying to get
Matthew and Beaumont to do their duties and help Ruth with the
supper dishes. Mildred came to the phone.

"What? No, he's left for the church. Said he had to drain the
baptistry and to read and do some preparations for Wednesday night's
meeting of the council. Is it urgent?"

By the time Thestal found his way into the doorway of the church study, the last few minutes of frantic phone tag had put the preacher in his swivel chair with his back to the door, talking on the phone to his wife with the message to call Lavola Briscoe as soon as possible. Mildred's voice as well as her words told him that Lavola was upset. "I think she's worried about Billy. Must have taken a turn for the worse."

But the preacher sensed that Lavola's call came from a different urgency. It meant trouble, no doubt; the kind of trouble that could see him forced out of Bethlehem Baptist, forced into long, church-sponsored counseling, and a move to another town. So soon. All so soon. All he said was, "Yes, I'll call her right away."

His finger touched the phone dial at the same time Thestal first squeezed the trigger. The slugs ripped into the preacher's lilac-smelling collar and neck in quick succession. Two tore into shoulder and back muscle and through his lungs, causing his once nicely ironed shirt pocket to blot up the flowing blood with the effect of an uncapped fountain pen used to record one columnar deficit after another in the church ledger. Thestal emptied the clip at the preacher's phone hand, the same hand that had led him down the baptistry steps into another life in that lifetime of a day ago on Sunday morning, the same hand that Pastor Ron remembered, in what was his last lightning flash of conscious thought, reaching up to hold Lavola's round, full, plum-blossom breasts.

Then, to the accompaniment of an incessant busy tone emanating from the phone receiver, Thestal picked up the limp body of Pastor Ron. The busy tone was sustaining, and Thestal began to hum, imitating the mechanical mindlessness of the noise. As he drew closer to the baptistry, the repeating monotone of Thestal's crazed ventriloquist hum changed, in his obsessed mind, into the caressing strains of Lavola's Sunday morning playing of "Softly and Tenderly." "Softly and Tenderly." He could hear Brother Herschel again. The water in the tank was calmed and inviting. The curtains were still drawn back and the empty sanctuary filled partially with the blurred faces of his glorious salvation as Thestal descended the baptistry steps and waded into the cold water with his burden. When his shoes felt the bottom he allowed the preacher's body to float out free. Almost lovingly, he arranged Pastor Ron's arms around his own sun-burned neck.

"Jesus is calling," he sang softly, "Calling, oh, sinner, come home," and Brother Thestal Briscoe took Pastor Ron Decker down with him into the bloody waters of the tank.

Glen had given old man Marshall the rubber waders to patch for the second time when Haskill rushed in with the morning news.

"I can't believe it. Found 'em both dead, floating in the baptistry at church. Pastor Ron was diddling Lavola and Thestal snapped when he found out."

The old man said nothing. He took an ice pick, the one he had used to puncture the new holes last time, and gouged the top of the metal-encased incendiary mixture seated over the hot patch. Then he slowly lit the match and applied it, through the fingers of the metal clamp, to the patch. As he watched it sizzle and smoke and smelled the sulfur of the combustion, he laughed. Then he turned his head slightly to the side and spit a long arc of tobacco juice through the smelly smoke into the tub of gray, putrid water used to test tires and tubes for leaks.

All Glen said was "Do you think Mildred will sell the old panel Chevy?"

REVELATION

WHAT TO DO ABOUT SKEETER'S SHYNESS? HOW TO MAKE HIM RECOG-
nize his talent and share it with the world without embarrassment? I
was taught by biblical parable to believe that if a person has a talent,
then that talent—especially a gift like Skeeter's—should have an audience, to inspire, encourage, just plain entertain. Blessings should
be repaid. They should be shared for the glory of God. Just think,
where would art be if there were no public expression of it?

If Skeeter were a painter or a pianist, then there would be no real
problem. But a shy singer? A singer so shy that the only way he could
sing was to cover his face with his hands, or his hat, or even a napkin,
for Christ's sake? There was good reason to get Skeeter to perform
onstage. He was good, damn good. Besides, I could see, even in
those early days, that there was money to be made! I didn't realize it
then but Skeeter turned out to be my first client. With him I turned my
own God-given instincts into the business I've built today. I've got
money now, and I owe Skeeter some credit for pointing me in the
right direction. In helping him I helped myself—the basis of a good
deal.

He had a voice born to sing lovesick country blues and could sing
just about any country-western song as if Hank Williams or Carl
Smith or Jim Reeves or any of the other greats were singing there in
the cafe, in person, right in front of you. I recognized right away that
if Skeeter could shed his shyness he could be a neighborhood star, a
larger living legend; a legend I knew as a friend and as a new person I

could maybe help create, although I didn't fully recognize it in that way then.

We would all try to coax him into a song when he was seated at the counter having his familiar root beer float or finishing a hold-the-onions hamburger. I started carrying extra nickels just so I could treat him and feed the similarly voracious jukebox. It didn't matter which song you chose on the counter jukebox menu, not at the M&M Cafe anyway. They were country-western songs for the most part, with maybe a rhythm-and-blues selection or two thrown in. Fats Domino could get Skeeter to tapping his foot. And Little Richard could evoke a whispered "Good golly" or two. But Skeeter lived for country-western music.

I would select a good country tune, drop in a nickel, and Skeeter would start to hum. Then, if everybody acted like they weren't paying any attention, he would start singing with Hank or Marty, Lefty, Webb, or Ernest. He could even augment the Western harmonies of a more sedate group like the Sons of the Pioneers. Ballads were his best. But he could do Western swing too. You wouldn't believe his rendition of "Take Me Back to Tulsa" or "Walking the Floor over You."

But as soon as he broke into the lyrics, down would slide his black-brimmed hat over his dark eyes, or up would go his hands, muffling all those beautiful sounds trying to get past the interference, sounds coming from who knows what more ethereal source than the counter at the M&M. I used to find myself just watching his Adam's apple, convinced I could see his vocal cords resonating with the wings of angels—all the way back to the perfections of Eden.

Maybe Skeeter's hat-over-the-face routine had something to do, in that mythic distance, with the fall of man. Maybe it was a version of the embarrassments of the fig leaf. I started wondering about things like that, wondering why in Sam Hill he couldn't just sing out loud and bold, started wondering if I could maybe straighten Skeeter out.

He knew the lyrics to just about every song out or soon to be released. He listened to the radio all the time in his truck. I knew that for certain because he had all the buttons punched for country stations. And I couldn't help but notice, on those first rides with

Skeeter, the songbooks strewn on the seat, and some others sun-curled on the dash. He would spend spare minutes jotting down lyrics in the cafe when a new record appeared. He would make requests with Betty Jo and Vivian, the waitresses, and with Mitch, the owner, head cook and bottle washer, and big Money Man (as he always identified himself). Skeeter would even hang around until the juke-box man came by to change the tunes. Then Skeeter would ask for favorite songs and jot down new titles.

Besides Ernest Tubb's "Walking the Floor over You," Skeeter loved "Lovesick Blues," and when Hank would stop after the chorus and let his band have it, Skeeter would keep right on going, yodeling "Oh, Lord" and all. I was convinced he was just as good as Ernest Tubb and old Hank and a kind of blend of the two. But Skeeter's talent went beyond imitation. We all sensed that he just needed some original material. If he could only rid himself of his infernal shyness. He would start to sing and I would start to think, "What if I could maybe get him to the attention of some of the local country-western bands? How could I help break the shyness?"

Soon I started to formulate a plan: First, get him to sing in front of everybody at the M&M; then convince him to enter the newly opened Esquire Theater's upcoming talent show—actually set foot on a stage. Get him to take his hat away from his face, and face not just an audience but himself and his ability to entertain people, to give them some happiness.

While I was working on staging some real performances for Skeeter, I would try to find the cause of his shyness and in so doing discover the cure. I would "stage" stage fright, help him conquer it, and then Skeeter would be on his way to a career as a country singer.

You must understand, I was about sixteen or seventeen at the time. Just a kid. All this curiosity and motive from a kid. What I didn't fully realize was that in my attempts to create a new Skeeter, or re-create him, I was creating a new me, finding what turned out to be my calling. I can't fully explain why I took it upon myself to cure Skeeter of his shyness by forcing him onstage, by attempting to find the root of his embarrassment, becoming detective and confidant along the way.

By the time I formulated my plan I thought I knew him pretty well. I didn't. And I'll be the first to admit that before I became so obsessed with his inhibition to sing in public I was interested in him mainly because of Janet, his sister. (She pronounced it "Janét," not just "Janet," like most people would say it.) When I first saw her I thought she was Skeeter's girlfriend. She would usually pick him up after school in his much-faded and filmy-white V-283 El Camino or buzz him by the M&M. She would get out only to take the wheel, if Skeeter had been driving. She would never come into the cafe with him. All Skeeter would say was that she was off to work. Seems like she worked the night shift. I never thought too much about it—at first.

Or she would wheel up to the curb on Broadway by the high school, and he would say a quick good-bye to the gang and jump in. Off they would go with glasspacks growling, headed north, windows down and wind blowing through her long, glistening black hair. I came to find out that they lived in a three-room house out on Second Street with their mother. I found out some other things too—about their growing up, about their parents, about Janet's job. Sure, my curiosity about Skeeter and my own curious need to cure him ran the risk of being nosy. But it was a risk, revealing as it was in the end, that was more than worth the taking.

When I found out from Larry Bodenstein, one of our mutual pals, that Janet was Skeeter's sister and not his girlfriend, I knew that I could get Larry or Skeeter to introduce me to her, enjoy her beauty and allure close up. Larry had a crazy crush on Janet and called her his Filipino baby for some strange reason, associating her with the lyrics of another country song in those days, which became, for Larry, Janet's theme song. "Her father came from Texas and her ma from Arkansas," Larry would repeat again and again, amid Cheshire cat grins and the gyrations of swiveling hips and "boom, boom, booms."

She did have a dusky, sensuous look, one that made you want to run away with her to some goddamn seedy Mexican town. It was a look that seemed, to me, more Mexican or Indian than Filipino. I knew from their surname that Janet and Skeeter's father was His-panic. Skeeter Sanchez was an odd kind of Americanized name. But it sure fit him—and everything fit Janet, as Larry would say.

To see her walk around the front of the El Camino at the M&M would leave me thirsting for more than the mustard and mayonnaise and carbonated fizzes of Mitch's hamburgers and fountain drinks. Janet was on the slim side, and tall. She always wore new Levi's and long, silver hoop earrings, hanging from pierced ears that she had done herself with ice cubes, hydrogen peroxide, and a sewing needle, a legendary detail I picked up in conversations with Larry.

I had never seen a cowboy shirt look better on anybody. The tapered cut, an open top snap or two, the white cotton—all emphasizing her tanned neck and beautifully contoured breasts. She had a low-class wantonness about her, a worldliness that threw me into taboo thoughts and teenage lusts. I imagined her as a model—a deep-copper beauty—who could cinch a job for some illustrator assigned to do an erotic "ethnic" cover for a Western paperback. In my own stylized, illustrated fantasies I would rescue her from whatever perils she faced and receive my rewards in her arms. Or, more down to earth, I would be that illustrator, taking countless preliminary photos and making numerous rough sketches.

Once I started asking some questions about Skeeter and Janet, I discovered plenty of rumors and uncovered much willing and wild gossip. Phil Parker told me that Janet had been in a bad car wreck spring before last on the way back from a drinking party at Doc Long's picnic grounds east of town in the mountains. Jerry Gibbon had been at the wheel, both of them drunk, and only his father's money was able to keep the drunk-driving arrest out of the papers. Phil said just to look for the scars on her ankles and legs. Check the May 18, 1959, obituaries for the name of the old man they killed. Betty Chapin said she knew for a fact that Janet had gone to Kansas City for an abortion and that Skeeter had taken her there on the *Santa Fe Chief*. Mannie Velasquez just said it was the dad, old man Sanchez, that caused the trouble. I started to file away these kinds of rumors for whatever bearing they might have on Skeeter's shyness.

One day I was lucky enough to get a ride with Janet and Skeeter from the M&M to my house over on Isleta Place, not far from the Esquire theater. Janet was surprisingly easy to get to know. Called me Frank right away and said for me to call her Janet. And, hiding my pounding heart and stammering tongue and a disbelief at her flirtations with me, I complied. That was the real beginning of things starting to fall into place.

The Esquire had only been open about two or three months. It was a classy neighborhood theater with a big, superbright marquee, a big, nicely carpeted lobby lined with mirrors and long candy and popcorn counters, and the newest in projection and sound equipment—ready for 3-D movies, CinemaScope, hi-fidelity speakers, you name it. Janet was driving the El Camino, and when we passed the theater billboard advertising the Saturday afternoon talent show, I said, "I'm going to enter you in the talent show, Skeeter. What do you say? We can get Art Kibben to play for you—Art and Curly?"

Skeeter laughed and, shaking his head, started to say, "No," but before the inevitable refusal Janet's approval of the idea came faster. "Sure, Skeet, you could win. And those guys would play for you. I know how good they are. I'll talk to them."

By that time we pulled into my driveway and I was out of the truck, pointing toward Skeeter and telling him, "You're on, Skeeter! You're on a week from Saturday! Skeeter's Saturday."

Janet simply said, "Yes, Skeet, I'll help you. Frank, I'll ask Art and Curly and we'll both work on Skeet here."

The light of her smile and her expression made me almost ignore her words. But somewhere in the midst of my total attention to the way she looked, her words of encouragement registered. And after a shower and a quick supper with my family I walked over to the Esquire office and signed Skeeter up to sing in the following week's talent show. The first-place prize was twenty-five dollars, a year's free "admit one" pass to all Duke City theaters (including the Esquire), and a photo in the *Tribune*. It was Thursday. I had ten days to turn the first phase of my plans for Skeeter into reality.

Art Kibben and Curly Weems were part of a country band called the Cactus Cowboys, which played regularly around town, but especially at the Palomino Club. Art was blind and didn't wear any dark glasses, so it was a bit hard, at first, to talk to him. He was in his late twenties and lived a pretty wild life for a guy with his handicap. Some say it was the fast living that caused the blindness. At my tender teen age I had never heard him play onstage at any of the clubs. But he came in the M&M and I knew him that way, over meals and such, and by reputation as the city's premier lead guitarist. Word was, he could sing decently too, had a way with lyrics and could make you feel them. So I called him up and asked him if he was willing to rehearse a song or two with Skeeter and maybe back him up in the talent show. I marvel today at my courage; me, a kid calling up the leader of the Cactus Cowboys as if I wanted him to play softball on my after-school team.

He said, "Sure. Janet mentioned it to me. We'll do it for her and for Skeeter. You're not horning in on any prize money are you, kid?" I assured him of my good motives and uttered a loud "Yes!" when I hung up. Art's yes meant Curly would come too. Curly pretty much looked after Art and drove him around to all the bars for gigs and other kinds of partying, in addition to playing a wailing steel guitar.

A trio of *música del oro* singers from Armijo won the Saturday talent show. I went to check things out and saw a pretty good movie too—*Seven Brides for Seven Brothers,* a musical with Howard Keel and Russ Tamblyn. I got so excited when I thought of actually seeing Skeeter up there on the Esquire stage—and the stages awaiting him, and me, beyond that—that I ate two boxes of popcorn and a Butternut bar.

The first part of the week I spent making sure Mitch would let us set up for rehearsal. He knew it would mean extra business and was all for it. Wednesday evening found Art's band setting up at the M&M for an 8:00 P.M. practice session. Art and Curly brought two other musicians—a drummer and a bass player—ready to play whatever songs Skeeter chose. We plugged in the amplifiers, arranged the microphone and chairs, ordered Cokes—and looked for Skeeter and Janet to come through the door.

The place was starting to fill up, and Mitch was demonstrating how he got his and his cafe's name. He was always happy when business came in and the register started ringing. That and people's voices were the best music to his ears. He could walk around with a dishtowel over his shoulder and say, in an assumed New Yorker accent, "For you, a deal. Just for you, sweetheart." He was working the counter and tables in his fake New Yorker style, along with Vivian, who was working for tips like the radiant and unassuming

Tennessee hillbilly she was. Betty Jo was fry cook, sizzling behind the counter. As for me, I was beginning to worry.

At 8:20 Skeeter and Janet were yet to arrive. So Art and Curly tuned up and started to play a couple of songs. Curly began with a long version of "Steel Guitar Rag," and Art followed that with "San Antonio Rose." He felt a lot. His eyes rolled back into his head and, it sounded like, his heart, because the feeling of the song could be "seen." He even turned his head toward the front parking lot a couple of minutes before the time when, with everybody's greeting, Skeeter and Janet actually came in the door to the sounds of Curly's swinging an upbeat "My Adobe Hacienda."

The brother and sister resemblance was more obvious to me than ever; their family features were highlighted by their Western, free-spirited look: roughed-out, buckskin-colored boots, dark-blue new Levi's, two-and-a-half-inch belt with rodeo buckles. Janet had on her dangling earrings and a loose, scarlet scarf; Skeeter wore an inlay bolo tie and his hat, freshly brushed. Janet's hips were alive with all the energy and excitement of the night. I stood momentarily mesmerized. Art finished the final chorus of the song, and Curly motioned Skeeter over to the band. They talked for a while, and then Skeeter was standing before the microphone. The cafe crowd quieted down some, and Art started a lead-in riff to "Satisfied Mind."

Skeeter didn't sing much Porter Wagoner stuff, and he gave this song an interpretation all his own—what you could hear of it. Right away he started to flush and ripen into the color of Janet's scarf. He tried to adjust the mike and then mispronounced a word. Then came a nervous cough. That sent his hand to his hat, and down the brim started to come about the time he hit the words "It's so hard to find one rich man in ten . . ." He was able to finish the song, but the crowd was about as embarrassed as Skeeter was.

Janet kept looking right at him, however, never turning away, never seeming to be embarrassed for him or for herself. She was the first one to start applauding when he finished—then she sprang forward to give him a hug. Then we all chimed in and Roscoe Daring cried out, "Sing us another one, Skeeter. Do Jim or Hank."

Skeeter slid his hat back up his forehead, and I noticed, because it pulled back his hair, that his hairline was much higher than I had realized. His scalp was sweating and his right hand choked the mike stand with a white-knuckled grasp. This time Art stood beside Skeeter at the mike and Curly, his boot slapping the tile floor, began an up-tempo, sliding-note lead into "I'm in the Jailhouse Now." It was to be a duet, thanks to Art's sensibilities, and he sang the first verse, with Skeeter joining in on the chorus. Mitch roared when they reached the part about "playing cards and shooting dice and getting drunk on Sunday," and Skeeter was fine until it was his turn for a verse.

Down came the hat again! Art kept strumming out the fancy chord changes on his big twin-pickup, push-button Epiphone. And they ended with another chorus together. After that the band took a break. Janet and I congratulated Skeeter. And we all thanked Art and Curly and the band. Curly chimed in with the suggestion that all Skeeter needed was a guitar to hold. And Art said with a laugh as serious as any I've ever heard, "Skeeter, why don't you just sing with your eyes closed like me?"

It hit me with the force of revelation. "Get him to sing with his eyes closed—or just buy him sunglasses." After the crowd thinned out, Skeeter went over "I'm So Lonesome I Could Die" about six or seven times, and he reached the point where the brim of his hat rested on the top of his eyebrows, not over them.

"Look inside when you sing; close your eyes like me," Art would say now and again. By Saturday I was confident I would have Skeeter singing with his eyes closed, wearing shades and holding a guitar, even if he didn't know or couldn't see the right chords. He could just hold tight to the damn thing and keep his hands away from his hat.

Art told me that I could rent a guitar at Bernie's music store downtown and told me to see Bernie or Harold Stone. So after school the next day I walked downtown and went into Bernie's. I asked for Bernie first, but he was upstairs doing paperwork. Bernie's store manager, Harold ("call me Hal") Stone, introduced himself as a friend of Art's too. When I explained the situation he showed me an inexpensive Gibson flattop, sunburst finish, and said I could have it "as is" (no new strings) through the weekend for ten dollars, including insurance. As he was finding a cheap soft-shell case, Stone said, "For Skeeter Sanchez, eh—Fillimino's boy? That old *borrachon* was a hard case," and Stone apologized for the cruel humor. "He was the only guy I knew always to be more stoned than me," and he laughed again at his clever cruelty.

I started putting things together. More revelations! And I said, "What happened to Mr. Sanchez? Skeeter and Janet live with only their mother now, don't they?"

"Well, the part of the story I know isn't pretty. Fillimino was a pretty good accordion player—you know, at all the church fiestas and fund-raiser dances. That's where he met Linda, at the Atrisco fiesta. I know because I was there; new to the state, of course, but I was there. One of my early calls to play drums when I first started to work for Bernie. Those two made a good-looking couple and after an exchange of a few impassioned glances, Fillimino set down the squeeze box and went out under the tent, on the board floor and asked Linda to dance. It was a lovely sight, the two of them: young, full of life, their blood pulsing to the Mexican polka.

"You guessed it. They were married. Had the two kids. But by then Fillimino was a bona fide wino. He would beat up Linda—and some say the kids too—and finally he just left them. Left town and left them to their own resources. Word came from around Barstow that he was killed by a freight train. Tried to jump it while drunk. Fell under the wheels. Linda had no education. Worked for a while as a cafeteria cook in the public schools. Janet was the oldest and started working right away. Did you ever see her perform? Get her onstage at this talent show of yours and I guarantee she'd win. Know what I mean?" And he laughed his own rehearsed, supersalesman laugh again.

I thanked him and took the guitar. Just as I reached the door, in walked a guy about six-one or so—pretty tall guy—with another man, closer to my height, dressed in a great-looking California-style suit. The tall guy was none other than Tex Ritter. I recognized him, with a stunned openmouthed expression, as Tex Ritter. He partially tipped his high-crowned hat to me and called me partner or something. And I remember thinking that one of these days that might be me and Skeeter promoting a new record at some big store in Denver or someplace. And I remember thinking as I walked down Central and then down Fourth Street to Coal and the bus stop, that I sure would like to hear Janet sing. For singing, I assumed, was her talent, just as it was Skeeter's. For some silly reason I pictured her singing with Skeeter, or Tex Ritter or Rex Allen or somebody, and me right there in the wings counting out a fistful of bills. I was finding out much and learning some possible causes and cures for Skeeter. But, bouncing across the Barelas Bridge on the bus, I had no way of knowing just how falsely smug I was in my reveries of Janet's mellifluous voice and how Skeeter would win the talent show.

Val Mondragon, a local Spanish radio announcer and personality, made the introduction with a glitzy kind of border accent: "And now we have Skeeter Sanchez from North Second who will sing 'I'm So Lonesome.' His backup band is Art Kibbens and the boys from Palisades and the Palomino Club. Give him a hand and take it away . . . Skeeter Sanchez. *Vámanos!*"

Val applauded a couple of times, trying to lessen the whine of the mike feedback and contouring his arms so as not to mash his notes as he backpedaled into the wings while the curtain went up. There, onstage, in living color, was Skeeter, with hat, sunglasses, and guitar. Art stood close by and Curly wasn't standing much farther back, playing a Dobro and not a steel—a last-minute try for a bluegrass effect. The drummer and bass player and others filled in the back of the stage. Janet was front row center again, next to me. I crossed my fingers as Skeeter started to sing. The mike level was great and Art knew how to play with just the right volume to give Skeeter the assurances he needed. Skeeter mimed the chords on his guitar; but no one but a guitarist could tell it. Skeeter kept it up. Kept singing! Janet reached over and grabbed my hand and squeezed it hard all through the rest of the song. And he made it all the way through—loud and proud. He made it through three verses and two choruses, and then Art's band brought it to a mournful arpeggio close. The curtain fell and the theater crowd whistled and cheered. Janet and I stood up to applaud and between a couple of excited jumps she reached over and kissed me on the cheek. We had to sit through a baton-twirling act and some guy trying to make a rope dance, and then Val came out again and juggled a couple of pages of his notes before announcing that Bobby Sisneros, the ventriloquist who had preceded Skeeter, was the winner. Big dummy deal!

Backstage with Skeeter I couldn't get too depressed, because he was happy that he had made it all the way through the song without reaching for his hat. In his jubilation he was a kind of winner. I could see that. And it was a beginning, a breakthrough for us to build on. So my spirits revived.

Curly spoke up, saying, "Let's get to the club. We're on at ten o'clock."

Janet was as happy as anybody and, turning to me and Skeeter, said, "Why don't you both come with us and we'll continue the celebration? Art can get you in, Frank."

So we all piled into Art's Monterey station wagon, instruments in the back, Curly driving, and headed out to Palisades and the Palomino Club. At that time I still didn't know what was in store.

I walked in with the band, with not even an attempt by the bouncer at the door to check my ID. Skeeter and Janet and I sat at a table close to the dance floor and the stage, which jutted out from some heavy curtains with glittering gold palomino horses on them. There was a comedian behind a mike telling some dirty jokes. But he was near the end of his act. Then Art and Curly and their band took over, augmented by a hot fiddle player and a Boots Randolph–type yakkity sax player. We ordered some beers and Janet excused herself, I guessed to go to the "powder room."

Skeeter was still pretty happy but curtailed his talk and started fidgeting with his hat and bolo tie. Out comes this comedian guy again, doubling as emcee and assisted by a couple of long snare drum rolls, he steps up to the mike and says, "And now, ladies and gentlemen, the featured act of the night—that beautiful, alluring, curvacious, most exotic of exotic dancers. Dancing here, tonight, for your entertainment and your enlightenment, direct from her recent triumphant shows in the Far East, far east at the Paradise Club out in the canyon—the Filipino Baby."

And there, onstage, in G-string and Palomino pasties, was Janet. I caught my breath and actually swooned at the shock and show and revelation of it all. Not fully recovered, I reached for Skeeter's hat to cover my face . . . just for an awestruck second, before pouring it full of foaming beer and ramming it back on his head while all my old taboo fantasies started to take on pulsing flesh-and-blood reality to the rhythm of Janet's bumps and grinds—the loveliest, most amazing artistry my young eyes had ever seen.

RYE WHISKEY

THEY MET FOR THE FIRST TIME ON THE SIDEWALK OUTSIDE THE EL Fidel Hotel. Some of Hop's band members were huddled on the corner of Sixth and Central, laughing and talking to the accompanying heavy spin and whoosh of the hotel's glass revolving doors. The road-weary touring bus was idling, coughing black diesel smoke out the elevated tail pipe and trying to ready itself to head north—along Coronado's old route, El Camino Real, up the Rio Grande, through Bernalillo and over La Bajada hill—for its own royal entrance into Santa Fe and on to the armory for the dance.

The bus doors were open and the driver, Billy Burt McCurdy, was behind the wheel doing some last-minute napping before Hopwood and his troupe of musicians boarded. The knock and clatter of the big GMC motor worked as a syncopated accompaniment to Billy Burt's snoring. He had driven the biggest and the best, from Faron Young to Ferlin Husky. And not just on the road trips that over the years had crossed and crisscrossed the country. For two years he had been Bob Wills's personal driver and still wore his once-spiffy leather bow tie and gray wool black-billed cap to prove it. The tarnished brass shield pinned to the cap's latticed frame boasted a red-etched authorization: "Oklahoma Chauffeur, 0463-1949." He started driving for Arco Oil Company in Tulsa just after the war and met Bob Wills's sister one night at a Sand Springs bar. Another night "my brother Bob" needed to get to Joplin, and Billy Burt was there. The rest was material for his own embellished legend.

There was no destination registered on the scroll over the bus cab, not even a "Chartered" sign. But Troy Maxwell, the dapper young man striding in a cocky kind of modified goose step down the street toward the historic hotel's entryway, saw "Santa Fe" in bold, imagined letters. And, as he glanced in a plate-glass window and deftly stroked his glistening, Wild-Rooted hair, he saw, imposed over his reflection and the uniforms in Simon's Department Store, a phantom armory marquee announcing "Fiesta and Dance . . . HOP HOPWOOD BAND. Featuring Troy and the Troubadours."

What he saw in real letters, bannered in fancy purple-and-gold script along the dingy aluminum side of the bus, confirmed it for him. What he couldn't believe was happening was really happening. There, clear as Nashville neon, was the invitation to his future dreams: "Hop Hopwood and the Grand River Boys." And there on the back of the bus, painted in mud-spattered, dust-coated gray and brown was "Hopper," the famous stylized jackrabbit—Hop's logo. The rabbit was resting on its haunches, long ears drooped back ever so slightly, resting but ready to hop into action. In Troy's reverie, the bus and its rabbit and the route north up the king's highway would take him much beyond a fifty-dollar night and a warm-up slot for Hop Hopwood. There was Amarillo, Kansas City, St. Louis, Nashville, New York, and . . . Hollywood.

Like Coronado and his conquistadors squinting into the far horizon for a clearer view of imagined and real vistas, Troy stared again at the bedraggled dream bus, exhaled a long-held breath of excitement, then turned and motioned for his own band members, Eddie and Dan, to catch up. They were stopped by the traffic light on Fifth Street, standing on the curb craning back to look up at the marquee of the Kimo Theater with their own invented versions of wonderment.

There were only four of the Grand River Boys waiting as Troy's trio stepped up for introductions. Hop Hopwood wasn't there yet. But Troy had seen enough album covers and publicity photos on songbooks to recognize Hank Garwin, Hop's lead guitarist. Hank wasn't any Chet Atkins, not as hot as Billy Byrd, but he was legendary as the guy Hop always told, complete with a Bob Wills holler, to "pick it out for the Hopper, Hank." "Ahhh . . . haa . . . Hank, pick it out for the Hopper!" And there always followed those characteristic hard-picking, finger-slapping, string-bending solo licks, with more treble than any other guitarist or amp setting could imitate. And then Hop would invariably move down range from the Bob Wills falsetto to a bass chant of "Hop, hop, hopper," followed by a squealing hillbilly hog call: "Sooo, sooo, soouey!"

His first album, *Hopalong Cowboy,* pictured him on the cover dressed up like William Boyd, complete with star-studded leather wrist guards and doing a combined Tennessee two-step and country clog of his own devising. Since then he had promoted himself as "the Hopper" and was reputed to wear jackrabbit-leather boots. He always dangled a rabbit's foot from a top tuning key on his J-300, jumbo-flat-top Gibson. His live performances were marked by his whipping the crowd up into a frenzied line dance of his two-step/clog.

Troy hoped to see that—see Hop Hopwood in his jackrabbit boots hopping to the finger and amplifier magic of Hank Garwin, picking it out for the Hopper. Troy wanted to see just what kind of amp and guitar Hank used; legend was that it was a Fender dual reverb and a sunburst L-5 with a hole cut in the back. He wanted to be onstage with the Grand River Boys, be like them, sweating and smiling and feeling the electricity in his fingers and the arc of his voice through the microphone and out the speakers behind him and to the side—reverberating through the hall and out the hi-fi's and over the radios playing his own recordings in cars and in bedrooms and at teen hops all over the country.

Troy recognized the man standing next to Hank as Floyd Drus-kin, now on the charts and climbing with "Stolen Love." Hank played a wailing, sliding arpeggio on that cut. Up until about a year ago, Druskin was unknown as a country singer. One blurb in a monthly lyrics magazine profiled him as an auto mechanic "discovered" in a Nashville club one night by an MGM scout. Troy estimated that he and Druskin were about the same height, about five feet eleven. But Druskin had a heavy beard line around his cheeks and over his upper lip, accented by a gap-toothed smile showing tobacco-stained teeth. He looked a bit like Popeye's nemesis, Bluto. Troy's face still had the handsome aquiline lines and high-cheekbone contours of a nineteen-year-old—no ravages of time or scarring from physical blemish or injury. His eyes were clear New Mexico blue and his anticipation as fresh and as high as the air atop the nearby Sandia Mountains. If Glen Campbell could do it so could Troy.

The other two musicians Troy didn't recognize, but he thought one was Curly Thoms, who, according to the fan magazines, did a lot of studio work and played steel guitar with some of the biggest Nashville recording stars, including Little Jimmy Dickens, Webb Pierce, and Lefty Frizzell. The other guy, with his foot propped up against the hotel wall and with drumsticks in his hands, was no doubt Tim "Tiny" Frazer, whose methods books were much in demand. Troy could see by Dan's expression that he recognized Tiny too.

It was Hop's band for sure—the Grand River Boys. Who else would be wearing maroon, Western-yoked, pearl-snapped satin shirts? Who else would be standing in front of the El Fidel waiting to board Hopper's bus? Not the Albuquerque Boys' Choir. There was no bass player, no fiddler that he could see, but he knew these four were the heart of Hop's band, out of Nashville, on a road tour through Texas and the Southwest—musicians who lived the life he hoped one day to live. He saw more dazzle and gleam on Hop's road-worn bus than was ever really there, except perhaps in the beginning days when Harold Horton Hopwood signed his first record contract and bought the bus from Cowboy Copus and christened it and himself "Hopper." Troy had Hop's history straight from the fan magazines.

With star-struck eyes Troy glanced up at the driver, McCurdy, decked out in his trusty leather bow tie as black as his brittle wisps of slicked-back hair, and Troy caught a strange, bemused, but not fully understood, look on his face.

"And who do we have here?" he seemed to ask. "And will you have your own bus and driver someday, complete with bug-splattered Tennessee plates? Or will you, like so many other horned toads, grasshoppers, and sundry varmints, splatter along the road-kill route to fame and fortune?"

Eddie and Dan caught up with Troy just in time to hear him say to Hank Garwin, "Excuse me . . . I'm Troy Maxwell, and this is Eddie Gallegos and Dan Crittendon, my drummer and lead guitarist. We're Troy and the Troubadours. We're booked to play the Santa Fe armory and the fiesta dance with you."

The beefy fellow, surrounded by a strong bay rum after-shave aroma and sporting a shower-shiny forehead, was the first to extend his mechanic's hand and say, through pillars of smoke and the bouncing rhythm of a cigarette magically stuck to his lips, "Floyd Druskin's the name. You're the local warm-up group, right?"

"Yah, that's us," Eddie and Dan said almost together, and shook hands with him.

Hank Garwin took a final couple of yellow-fingered puffs on his stub of a cigarette, dropped it on the cement, and smeared it into a blackened pulp with one of the most expensive-looking shoes Troy had ever seen, a low-hugging, tasseled suede loafer. "Pleased to meetcha, fellas," he drawled in what hit Troy's ear as a parody of southland talk.

" 'Troy and the Trojans,' is it?" he twanged and then looked over and winked at Druskin and his buddies. "Hop's still up in the room trying to learn to walk again. Say hello to the Grand River Boys. Hank here's greatest on G-string solos, Curly's an expert with Hawaiian hulas, and Tiny beats his . . . drums in all of two different tempos. Earl and Vern will be down with Hop."

"How did y'all line up this gig?" was Curly's question as he removed a curved, chrome finger pick and stuck out his hand.

"Why do you call yourself the Trojans? Are you always ready or built to last or what?" asked Tiny as he slid his sticks through his belt, grinned, and shook Eddie's hand.

"Troy and the Troubadours," Dan spoke up, "not the Trojans. We were just ready and available. It's a big break for us."

"That sounds pretty risky to me! How 'bout you boys?" taunted Hank and laughed a raspy laugh, preliminary to a cough and a long-arching, phlegmy spit into the street.

Just as the laughter subsided, a tall, teetering, ashen-faced specter, aided by two maroon-shirted cowboys, stumbled through the revolving doors and wobbled out onto the sidewalk. It was Hop Hopwood in real life!—down from the marquees and album covers and right out of fan magazines and the spinning front door of the El Fidel Hotel. The flesh and the blood of it: the Hopper!

He wore a beautiful Western-cut, dark-brown gabardine suit, set off by turquoise ribbing. One pant leg was tucked into his unusually

high boot top, the pulls sticking up in long-eared, jackrabbit prominence. His tan satin shirt was unsnapped at the neck and halfway
down his chest. He was trying to slide a leather bolo around his
turquoise neck scarf with about as much success as a palsied grand-
father trying to light an errant pipe.

Soon Hop's moving lips began to make slurring sense to Troy:
" 'If . . . the ocean was whiskey and I was a duck, / I'd dive to the
bottom and never come up. Rye whiskey, rye whiskey, rye whiskey, I
cry. / If I don't get rye whiskey I think I will . . . die.' Get my rock
and rye. Get my gee-tar. Get the shit away. . . ."

Hop twisted away from the supporting grip of his two cowboy
valets, hollered out a loud "Ahhh . . . haaa," and started playing an
imaginary guitar with extravagant jerks of his hands and neck,
kicking the air and stomping his custom-made boots on the sidewalk.
Soon he was jumping up and down in a pogo-stick series of unstable
hops that spun him into the side of the bus.

"Ahhh . . . I, I gotta piss, gotta piss . . . key! Shine, shave
and . . . San Antonio Rose, San Antonio Rose," he started chanting
as he wavered and bobbed toward the rear corner of the bus, one boot
on the curb, the other in the gutter, causing him to look like a forlorn
patient permanently deformed by a crazed orthopedic surgeon.

"What the hell, Hop," yelled Billy Burt, startled from sleep and
now leaning out the bus door, his cap in his hand, his feet on the first
rubber-covered step of the bus and his bug eyes staring back at his
drunken boss. "Grab him, you dumb asses. He's still shellacked all
to hell. Into his Tex Ritter imitation. No show, no dough, boys."

"Get him, Earl," spoke up Druskin with a sullen expression and
an exasperated tone. "The son of a bitch will piss all over hisself
right there on the street. That's the kind of press we need. He's
plastered worse than we thought."

But Hopwood had reached the end of the bus and stumbled into
the street, fumbling with his fly, his singing now become the gut-
aching wretch of the dry heaves. He threw up some greenish-yellow
bile, which stained his bell-bottomed suit pants and dribbled onto his
fancy boots. He reached out with both hands to lean on the bus,
on what happened to be the louvered engine cover, and, instantly
burned, fell forward, with first his wrist and elbow and then his head

clipping the bumper. Passed out, knocked out, barely breathing through the gurgle and the thickening stench of the liquids still in his mouth, Hopwood lay sprawled on the pavement, looking up through the blindness of his alcoholic stupor at Hopper, his painted jackrabbit mascot, seemingly panting to the tired, syncopated knock and clatter of the motor.

"Well, ain't it grand, boys. I hope you and Floyd are in good voice tonight, kid," quipped Hank as he looked into Troy's staring, sparkling, eyes which were already cast far past the fallen Hopwood and his droopy-eared jackrabbit to places and routes much distant from El Camino Real and the royal city of faith.

Against the bass line of the idling bus motor and the crestfallen realizations of Eddie and Dan, Troy Maxwell, the New Mexico troubadour, stroked his greased ducktail. He could already hear the glissando and the treble twang of Hank's guitar amplified over the armory crowd and could discern his own brave and bold electrifying command, "Pick it out for the kid, Hank. Pick it out for the . . . *KID*, Hank. Ahh . . . haaa!"

NEONATE

A new person is to me a great event and keeps me from sleep.
—Emerson

TONIGHT, MORE THAN EVER, I WANT MORE ARTISTRY IN MY SIGNS.
Thinking here, naked in the neon glow, about Carlotta and Doc and
Mexico and all that has happened shows me that my signs can be
works of art, can be sculptures even—at least I want them to be.
Why stay with signs? Why just light up names and logos on building
walls? Neon can be used inside too, displayed and enjoyed just like a
painting, watched and absorbed. The idea of bending light, of giving
it shape and color, of taking colors and designs out of life and then
reshaping them with different imaginative turns and hues and moods
and showing them to life again—well, that's neon. I think I'll do
Carlotta, the curves of her body as I've felt them and seen them—
nude in neon. Why not?

In Mexico there was no neon at night, and I craved it. Sure, the
sun was spectacular during the day, especially there on the boat,
fishing and joking around with Doc. Whether he realized it or not,
Doc and his idea of south-of-the-border fishing helped me understand neon and the need for it. The contrasts of sunny days and dark
nights, the spectacular fish, the dingy bars—and Doc's high-low
extremes—were . . . well, they were illuminating. Doc fathered
some of that. Maybe that makes me a son of that Mexico sun, and of
Doc and our times. Now I can see the whole experience, my friendship with Doc and my attraction to Carlotta, my own life, like one of
the designs I work up for my signs: the heat, the argon, the bending
and welding of the glass tubing. Is the neon father to the sign? Who

the transformer, the electrode, the electricity? Who in this neon strip
lit the sun?

Maybe all people see their lives through their work, see who they
are in or through what they do. For me, it's neon. For Doc it was
medicine, until things flickered and went out. There's much I don't
know and still can't piece together about his life and the turns and
twists that brought him to his final fate. Good and bad, in life and in
the glow of memory, Doc—the bastard—was quite a guy. I know
that fishing that time in Mexico with Doc, as I remember it, gave me
one hell of a charge. . . .

Most of the morning we trolled for yellowtail. No luck. Then we
anchored a few yards from some of the big rocks that splotched the
Guaymas shoreline. We were fishing deep off the side of the boat.
Later we would troll, "Un tiempo más," as Hernan put it. We would
try trolling again, but for Spanish mackerel this time. That was the
plan, such as it was. We weighted our lines, even tied on old
wrenches and pliers, and let the line spin downward into the darker
layers of water . . . and waited our time for red snapper, grouper, sea
bass—or maybe sharks.

"Hay tiburones aquí también," the two crewmen chattered, and
confirmed the warning with wrinkled foreheads and raised eyebrows:
"Mucho ojo hombres, mucho ojo."

Los payasos, we called those two guys. The clowns. The same
name could have been applied to me and Doc, I guess.

The hotel restaurant had shark steak on the menu. I remember I
didn't order any; I went for the shrimp scooped up live from a tank
where you could watch them propel themselves with short bursts
through the water. Later, that afternoon, we did catch mackerel—
"muchísimo mackerel"—as fast as we could reel them in. Doc was
having the time of his life—forgot about his sunburn and his captain's hat and counting the catch. It was pure joy for him, you could
tell. I had fun too, but I kept seeing Doc catching that shark and then
whipping out his pocketknife and slicing open its belly while he gave
me and the Mexicans a friggin' lecture on how to perform a Caesar-
ean section—on a still-living, gasping shark! We caught the mackerel in the afternoon, the red snappers and the shark in the morning.

After I saw Doc's surgery and what came out of the shark I was stunned for the rest of the day. I still see it vivid as all hell.

Fishing the deep waters off the side of the boat reminded me of the black distances and vast dimensions I sensed when, as a little kid (behind the park guide's tan-shirted back), I tossed a stone into a designated "bottomless pit" in Carlsbad Caverns. I waited forever by the carved wooden sign for the plunk into the watered wildness, imagining grotesque water monsters, their eyes long ago blind and useless, now disappointed that the intrusion was only a rock. I imagined the darkened sign, the water monsters' eyes, the whole damned Carlsbad Caverns lit up and luminous, phosphorescent—with neon. By the time the line ran out in Guaymas, however, the wait was over. You had a fish of some kind ready to drag up from the depths into the splash of salt water and sunlight. Try to pull up a couple of red snappers on one line from what feels like twenty thousand leagues under the sea.

"Full fathom five!" or some such Captain Nemo, Davy Jones gibberish, we would yell when the line ran out, maybe sixty or seventy feet down. And then we would set the lock on the reels and start "crankin' and yankin'," as Doc called it.

We were never quite synchronized—Doc and I—in our lives or in our fishing. That's what made spending time then with him such a damn charge. He would be cranking the reel and looking debonair like Gilbert Roland, bandana around his neck and shirt open on a hairy chest, waiting there at the oxygen hose for Robert Wagner to surface from a sponge dive in *Beyond the Twelve-Mile Reef,* and I would be baiting a goddamn hook with pieces of mackerel or shad or whatever the hell kind of fish it was we used as bait, or tying on another rusty wrench for more weight. But it was electrifying to watch Doc, to actually be with him there in Mexico listening to him toast the sharks and imitate famous sea dogs and fishermen, from John Paul Jones to crazed Ahab.

Doc was a combination professor and Toastmaster. In Guaymas, and on the drive there and back, he editorialized about everything under the mañana sun: more books I should read (he loaned books to me as fast as I could read them); the Mexican currency, politics, and poverty; Benito Juárez and Emilio Zapata; "música continental";

cactus species, exotic bar drinks, and gourmet Mexican food; the
Aztecs and their gods; Malinche, señoritas, señoras, streetwalkers,
strippers, prostitution, and venereal disease; bullfighting, cockfight-
ing, and the mystique of machismo; Montezuma—and his revenge.
Doc was sophisticated as all shit, and for a time I thought he was just
about the best. He had a pretty calloused attitude toward women,
though, and expressed it. Mexico was the first time it really registered for me that Doc didn't worship at the feet of women and
motherhood.

The fat fishing rods were pretty banged up, with a loose eye here
and there, but they worked. Work it was, too. Muscle-aching, sun-
burning work; but real fisherman fun to see snappers coming to the
surface, coral-pink and iridescent, with their eyes bulging and their
bodies twisting from the resistance and shock of it all. They were
water-slick and scaly, glistening on the boat floor there in the hot
redness and reflection of the Mexican sun. (Only later did they start
to smell.) I kept moving my sunglasses up and down for the pleasur-
able effect of changing colors and shadows and motion.

Doc certainly took the "field" of obstetrics to the extreme. He
said that pulling snappers out of the deep was something like de-
livering a baby. I guess that kind of talk got him thinking about an
"in-the-field" experiment with a pregnant sand shark. A lot of his
doctoring was as an "obstetrician," although he was an osteopath.
He had to straighten me out on the difference between obstetrics and
osteopathy.

The fish were biting as fast as we could hoist them up, too. No
worry about regulations, limits, or anything. All the talk about
catching sharks didn't really frighten me. The two Mexican jesters
were just putting an edge on things. Doc tried to keep it light,
although he'd wax philosophical, even morose and morbid once in a
while. His sense of humor took some turns down an unlighted street
or two of his own mind. I knew I was in deep waters with Doc in
more ways than one—just like I knew that these Gulf fish weren't
rock perch or crappie from Bluewater Lake, where I usually fished
back home.

All I had ever known was freshwater fishing. I liked to fish—and
had even fished and traveled and hiked some of the forty-eight: the

Rockies in Wyoming and Montana, fly-fishing for cutthroat and grayling and the more colorful, exotic trout. To see a trout rise to a well-placed fly on the Yellowstone in Wyoming or the San Antone in the Jemez Mountains of New Mexico is to see a beautiful combination of motion and color. The golden skin and pink meat of a cutthroat trout make it an especially colorful fish. The pink line along the sides of a rainbow trout jumping clear of the water for a strike makes you thankful for sight. Not even trout are as colorful as red snappers, though. Fishing—whether in cold mountain lakes or rippling trout streams, or there in the Gulf of California (the Sea of Cortez, Doc called it)—appealed to me in something of the same way that working with neon did, something glowing and vibrant. I came back from Mexico with new ideas about a neon fish for the Ute Grill. Doc said he would buy it if I didn't sell it to Warren Bills, who managed the place.

There in Mexico we dry-iced all the fish we caught and shipped them home to give to friends, gifts almost as welcome as a bottle of Gusano Rojo mezcal. That "hecho en Mexico" stuff made a big hit in the States. I bought a couple of bottles of mezcal, and Doc was already starting to call me Gusano. It fit, too, since everyone knew me as Gus anyway—Gus Smith. How my old lady chose a name like Gustav to go with Smith was always a curiosity to me. But I liked my name well enough, and sort of like Doc and me and positive and negative charges in the neon trade, opposites do attract.

I took all this "Gusano" stuff in the spirit of the outing, but who wants to be called "worm," for Christ's sake, especially on a fishing trip? We joked back and forth about all the possible meanings of a sunburned fisherman named Gus and nicknamed El Gusano Rojo. Doc the professor said fish and worms and reptiles and birds and whales and humans were all related through evolution. Sharks were prehistoric leftovers, according to Doc. He said that someday we should take a trip farther south to Ecuador and the Galápagos Islands, where Charles Darwin put together some of his theories about the survival of the fittest.

I got the point easily enough. The horned toad looked pretty damn old to me, and it was still around. And one time I saw a school of giant gar fish in Oklahoma. They were trapped in a pool below a dam where the water flow was cut off. Those long-snouted gar looked like they had for sure started out eons ago. It was a whole goddamn education to travel with Doc. You'd listen to him talk and suddenly things would start to make better sense, letting you connect something he said with something else you already knew, stretching and curving and connecting ideas like neon tubing. He said the salt in our body, our tears, and our sweat, gave more evidence to the saltwater origins of all life. He said that even the waters of the womb were salty!

He knew a whole hell of a lot, about birth for sure—and biology, and booze. Body chemistry, he called it. I kept picturing red snappers and sharks and ugly damn groupers and gar as ancient worms floating at the bottom of a very big, amniotic aquarium of mezcal—rimmed with salt. Conversations with him always took off in high-low, silly-profound directions. What eventually happened to Doc was part of that pattern, I guess. Everyone knew him as just "Doc," and I told him that I much preferred Gustav, my given name, to his Gusano razzing.

"Gustav Smith! Gustav . . . ," he repeated and snickered—and assumed this patronizing, arrogant pose, looking down his nose and acting prissy at the same time he cranked his reel with his little finger up and crooked, like he was having tea and crumpets in some London parlor.

"Very funny, Doctor Victor M. Hensley, D.O.," I said. "Better leave that 'Gusano' stuff for the Spanish mackerel, who can understand it," I fired back over his laughter. "I'll start calling you Doctor Hensley, you blue-blood son of a bitch. And tell the crew what the 'D.O.' stands for while I'm at it." That silly threat shut him up with strange haste.

Doc tried hard at being one of the guys. He was an elegant fellow, even when he put on adolescent airs and joked like that. In his bearing and dress and talk you could tell he came from an upper-class family: good breeding, good schooling. He said he worked his way through college back east by playing the saxophone in a dance band during and just after the Second World War. You can bet it was a private college and that he played the sax as much for fun as for work. Only a guy like Doc would call playing the sax work. Not me.

Not my old man, who never played anything or played at anything, not even fishing. He did nothing but carry around sacks of soiled sheets and laundry from hospitals and clinics and offices like Doc's to the plant, and then turn around and deliver laundered and sanitized stuff for the almighty employer: Excelsior Laundry and Dry Cleaning, Inc.

I realized that Doc was, in a way, taking his "son" fishing. But we were *compañeros* too, as they say down Mexico way. I grew up wanting to be someone like Doc, and not my dad. Working with neon never quite put me into Doc's sphere—the prestige and weight of science and saving lives. And yet, somehow there I was with Doc, driving across primordial deserts and fishing in historic Mexico, of all things. In some ways being a neon sign man saved my life, though, at least got me a bit farther along in the "life science" of survival than Doc was. Ironically, it was guys like Doc who kept me going to meet the day and see the change and coloration and charge of it all. Doc the neon sign!

Doc was entertaining as all hell when he started to mimic somebody we knew or some public personality, some star or celebrity, somebody from the movie or music worlds beyond ours. He could do a mean Vaughn Monroe or Bing Crosby with all the "Racing with the Moon" or "bobba bobba boo" flourishes, and then switch to Gabby Hayes, thrusting his chin out and pretending to talk, without teeth, to Roy Rogers and Trigger about the back forty or Miss Dale. A cool and hip Gabby Hayes in shades playing the sax would put me into convulsions. However, some of Doc's Gabby Hayes routines got pretty risqué. One or two about Trigger and Miss Dale were downright gross coming from a debonair, educated guy like Doc. Roy and Gabby as two cowboy fairies got pretty far beyond the pale, too. Then there was Gabby trying to eat his oatmeal in the smiling gaze of the Quaker Oats man. I wondered if Doc told dumb Gabby Hayes jokes after a nice dinner at the country club.

That day on the boat Doc stood up and acted like he was going to bleed the old lizard there in the water but just leaned overboard and poured out some of the long-necked Mexican beer he was drinking, then held the bottle high in a toast that seemed to me as cosmic as it was comic: "To Señor Gusano and Señor Tiburón . . . Roy!" Hernan, Raul, Doc—we all laughed at his lantern-jawed, raspy-throated Gabby Hayes: "The Pissin' Cowboy," skit.

"*Verdad, patrón.* You got her right. You do Señor Gabby good." And then old Hernan slid his pants down as low as he could until they were just hanging off his butt, grinned a ravaged smile, and proclaimed, "Yo soy Cantinflas! Viva Cantinflas and Señor Gabby! But por favor no say saludos to los charkas."

Hernan didn't realize how really crass a Cantinflas impersonator he was, which added a special kind of slumming, squalid punch to his performance. What he intended as A-1, Spanglish, please-the-tourists type of Guaymas entertainment somehow spilled over into a hodgepodge of pandering and wickedness.

Something wicked in Doc surfaced on that trip too, with him and Hernan performing the same low humor, the same "club," and working the same crowd, as it were. Bizarre as Hernan's and Doc's antics and lingo were, they were nothing like Doc and I saw later that night in the gyrations and mismatches of some local strippers when Doc said he knew where we could catch sight of a midget and a giant—and proved it with a twenty-peso cab ride to a smoke-filled Guaymas hot spot. For sure I wasn't one of those Victorian prudes or Puritans Doc harangued about, but Doc was starting to show his vulgar, shadowed side on that trip, as I now realize in more startling ways.

The brochures advertising Guaymas fishing, and word of mouth up north, had all advertised deep-sea sportfishing at its best: yellowtail, sailfish, and marlin. Hernan and Raul, his *hermano* first mate, told us when we rented the boat, and again when we left the docks, that we would land big, big fish. I knew I would land a yellowtail tuna or a sailfish twenty minutes out. Now *los dos payasos* tried a little too obviously to laugh at and imitate Doc's high jinks, and praise whatever we caught. Sure, we knew that our Mexican crew's desire for a successful outing translated into a potential *propina,* a bonus, so each "grande-muy-grande" celebration of identifying and sizing up just what kind and condition of fish we had snagged added to the fanfare and excitement surrounding what we pulled up. All the shark talk was just another tourist tactic—at first.

"Los gringos" didn't have to pretend to be excited. We were. The sunshine was luxurious in its brightness and heat. The water was light green at the top layer, then blue-green, and then darker green: beautiful in its colors and coldness. We had some iced soft drinks and ten or twelve bottles of *cerveza más fina.* The boat had all the look and rigging of a thirty-foot inboard yacht seasoned in battle. It was white with a blue cabin and had the name *La Pesquisa,* "the hunter," bannered across the stern. This was what the two-day drive was for. This was it! This was Mexico—vacation fishing in the Gulf of California.

Doc and I didn't know each other then the way we did later— until he ended it. That trip helped me understand the disappointment and I guess you could say shock of what I found out about what he was doing and how he wound up like he did. Thanks to that trip I couldn't wish him the devil's speed on his blackhearted way to perdition like so many people did.

Doc's little office (he referred to it as a clinic) wasn't in the best part of town; however, it was my side of town too. I thought he just wanted to help the poor, even though he led the good life in the Highlands district and belonged to the country club and all. His patients were not white-collar professionals. Mostly they were wage-earning, working-class people, especially women: wives, daughters, sisters—soon to be mothers.

His office was pretty close to the Ute Grill, where I always ate breakfast. And it was there, at the counter over ham and eggs and hash browns, that I first struck up a conversation with Doc. He found out that I did neon work, designed and made neon signs, and he hired me to come over and light his office. I usually did trim work, building borders and front-wall signs. I had never done any office windows before, let alone a doctor's office, but I was up to the challenge and needed the dough. After many bizarre ideas and possible designs, I finally fixed him a nice, refined, white-lettered sign (modeled some-what on my own tech-school diploma) for his front window:

VALLEY CLINIC
VICTOR M. HENSLEY, D.O.
FAMILY PRACTICE AND OBSTETRICS

If I were to make him a sign now—and at times I do in the glow of memory, flipping the switch every now and then—let me tell you, it wouldn't be a simple sign and it wouldn't be clinical white. The color and design would go back to that day in Guaymas waters when he caught the shark. Over time, that day and the Guaymas mood— the jagged and protruding shoreline rocks, the hunched and loitering buzzards in the palm trees, the two-hundred-mile shoot across the Sonora desert, and Doc's sand shark—all have become his "sign" in my buzzing, neon-flickering memory.

Doc owned a couple of racehorses and ran them at small tracks like Ruidoso Downs, and he would say between sips of *cerveza* on the boat or Cuba Libres back at the hotel, "You must go down to the Downs with me, Gus. That's our next trip. Down to the Downs."

About a month or two after I made his office sign and started to sit with him and Dexter, the potato chip salesman, and some other customers, over coffee in the Ute Grill, I went to him to treat a bad cold and he gave me a shot of penicillin, which cleared it up. That's when I first met his receptionist, Carlotta. Her Mexican-American good looks and welcoming personality gave me even more reason to start thinking of Doc as "my doctor." It was conversation about Carlotta that got Doc to planning the trip to Guaymas in the first place. She was a little plump. But she was voluptuous too. She was just naturally alluring, earthy, and looked like the uninhibited, animal type you would do just about anything for in bed if she asked you to— and then return the fun and the favor with interest while demonstrating how it *could* be done. But she seemed something less than a salt-of-the-earth mother: a bit bovine, cowed too, childlike, aiming to please, servile. Doc said she was a good receptionist and took orders well. Innocent me. Little did I realize then that she was willing to "play doctor" with and for Doc in robotlike, surprising, and finally tragic ways. I didn't think two shakes and a hoot about Doc and her being sexually, let alone criminally, involved with each other then.

Doc was, I guessed, almost ten or twelve years older than I was. I was twenty-six then, and I thought he was in his late thirties, maybe even forty. I went to the state college for a time and then quit and went to vocational school to learn a trade and keep myself together. I did some apprentice neon work in a sign company downtown before I decided to buy a little shanty of a house out in the Valley on Tapia Road and turn it into my shop (I thought of it as my studio). I just walked into the Merchants' Valley Bank one morning and convinced Chris Salazar to float me a small loan for everything—house and lot, gas and tubing, burners and tables, and other items of the trade. My first commercial neon sign was for my business there at the "studio":

"NEON SIGNS"

I decided not to make it too extravagant. I wanted to say, "Gustav Smith, Neon Artist" or something like that but decided against it. "Neon Signs" was what I came up with . . . but with the flair of some filigree bordering. I rigged it so that it flashed off and on, first in one fixed splash of colors, then in a running, sequenced series of colors, advancing up the spectrum of the rainbow. I was trying for the effect of a double rainbow. That ghost echo, plus the reduced redundancy of "Neon Signs" done in neon would leave a lasting image to anyone with eyes to see. "Signs by Rainbow Man" was another logo I considered. I saw myself as a kind of rainbow man. But I didn't want to get too explicit about it.

I liked the obvious curvaceous enticements of Carlotta a lot and wanted to see how far her welcome went. And aside from the monied contacts and possible contracts that association with Doc meant, he and I both liked each other well enough to plan and then take this little junket down south of the border. He was married, but I knew nothing about his wife other than as a ghostlike Mrs. Hensley. Doc would mention his wife, Mrs. Hensley, mostly in connection with their racehorse hobby. I got to know more about that and other things, and it wasn't too respectable. Apparently Mrs. Hensley liked the jockeys better than she liked Doc. And Doc preferred Carlotta and his women patients.

Anyway, after whirlwinding through Gallup, Flagstaff, Phoenix, Tucson, the border crossing at Nogales for inspection, and opening up Doc's big cream-colored 1958 Lincoln convertible through the desolation of Sonora around Hermosillo, we got to Guaymas and checked in at El Rincon Hotel. Doc chose it because of its "European" plan and villas. He knew about such things. Liked the good life. It was a classy place, too. Pulling up in front in Doc's Lincoln automobile (we cruised across the Arizona and Mexican deserts at 80 and 90 miles per hour) was so swank I couldn't believe it. We took a two-bedroom suite, and for just a paltry amount of *dinero* had all the perks: catering, cocktails, concierge, valet garage, room service, even complimentary safety deposit boxes. Doc took one for reasons known only to him at that time. He wore a snazzy Girard-Perregaux wristwatch, and he liked to carry a turquoise money clip of big bills and a sinister-looking pearl-handled knife in his pocket. So, down Mexico way especially, he had plenty of stuff to stow.

"Pharmaceutical supplies, my boy," was all he said. It was the fanciest hotel I had ever checked into. What I really grew to dislike about El Rincon and Guaymas, however, and just couldn't get used to as romantic or exotic or anything alluring like that, were the damn buzzards, outright vultures perching in the palm trees off the balcony. Those birds were all over Guaymas and gave the appearance of just coming in off the desert, like Doc and me, for a bit of rest and relaxation. Speeding across the Sonora sands, I caught sublime glimpses of black birds riding the thermals. And I thought of them again, subliminally, when Doc set up appointments with some of the seediest looking medical "colleagues" you could imagine.

They were fucking abortionists too, I later realized. But there in the Sonora the "joke" hadn't turned sick and ironic yet.

"Something circling at twelve o'clock, Doc," I said. "Just like in the movies, right? Is the water bag full?"

Doc, with his left hand out in the rushing, dry air stream, had a preoccupied, distanced look in his eyes. Then came a delayed smile, and he said in a voice I just caught over the wind sounds, "The wages of the womb is death, Gus," and I felt the Lincoln surge ahead to a new notch of speed.

Doc was a suave dresser! Good brands. Expensive clothes. Tasteful, not gaudy. On our deep-sea expedition he had on his canvas deck shoes, a white Izod shirt, and a pair of khaki Bermuda shorts showing gorilla legs. The captain's cap he bought at the marina, before we sallied forth that morning, set off his mustache and made him look dapper but a little touristy, I thought—like the caricatured *Esquire* magazine squire. Except Doc's mustache wasn't blond and bushy. His was black and neatly shaved in hairline precision, more like Gilbert Roland and Zachary Scott—you know, the swashbuckler, swordsman type.

He was a little too portly to be, finally, mistaken for a leading man. He was developing a little paunch and his cheeks seemed all the more fleshy because of his thinning hair. (The prominence of his cheeks and nose made them sunburn first thing.) He still could part it in the middle and comb it back to give him that dashing look, though. Over a martini back at El Rincon, and going into the dining room for dinner in his blue blazer and white slacks, he caught both the señoras' and the señoritas' eyes. He had white skin and a heavy beard, which made him look all the more intriguing—a look of gentility but with something of a down-and-out undercurrent to it.

He made a habit of shaving twice a day but still had a perpetual nine o'clock shadow. As a result of so much practice, he could shave with very little mess. A brush and a cup of soap for lather, a towel to serve as a bib around his neck, hot water, a washcloth, and a sharp razor and he was in business. He kept a couple of old-fashioned straight razors with carved ivory handles in his travel bag but usually just used a Gillette double-edged razor. He was the kind of guy who could shave without taking his shirt off. That was part of his style. What made Doc who he was. He was good with a razor and a scalpel too and said half seriously, "Good barbers made good surgeons."

The way he sliced that shark straight down the belly right there on the deck, with the boat rocking back and forth, and all the while coolly talking about his last operation made me lightheaded and then a little nauseated. A bit scared too. His knife wasn't a regular pocketknife. It was a butterfly knife with three inches of hard steel protruding at one swift squeeze of his hand! He was engrossed in his fancy knife work and applying pressure along the sides of the shark, but I guess he saw how wobbly I was.

"You ain't no Carlotta, kid. Opening. . . , closing. . . , or disposing—she never blinks an eye."

Given his fastidiousness in dress, it was a bit surprising to find out that as a doctor/fisherman he wasn't afraid to get his hands dirty. When he first realized that he had hooked a shark, he hollered sternly, "Hernan, don't clip the line. I want to land it and experiment."

Doc had all our attention then for a more serious kind of show. We saw the shark come to the surface, struggling and swimming wildly on Doc's line. The tip of his pole had a good bend in it and

Doc was pulling and reeling with a different kind of motive. It was complex, I guess. The shark was a patient and the shark was Doc.

Raul held the gaff hook with white knuckles and yelled, "Tiburón de arenal! Sand chark, patrón. Cuidado—be careful."

The shark was only about four or five feet long when we finally got it on the boat. Charcoal-gray and slick and tired from its struggle, it didn't look as monstrous as it had in the water, or in my imagination. Raul had the gaff hook in the side of its head and you could tell it was almost as good as dead. I actually felt sorry for the thing.

"Watch this, muchachos," was all Doc said as he kneeled down, turned the shark on its back and went to work with his sinister knife. Hernan and Raul sobered into silence and gave themselves a good Catholic crossing when they saw first one, then another, and another baby shark pop out of the mother's belly, Doc threw a baker's dozen of them, one by one, over the railing of the boat. They were alive and swimming and gone. Judging by Doc's expression and the pursing of his lips, he was completely absorbed in the surgery.

Doc would now and then say something about vivisection, viviparous births, and talk pretty fragmented and technical. With the beer, the sun, and the excitement I pretty much blanked out for a time and didn't get all the connections with just what he was saying and what he was trying to prove or verify. It was just that there, for me, the reality of Doc's work as a crazed kind of "obstetrician" hit home.

But it was Doc's suicide a year or so after the Mexico holiday that really laid me low. And has for the longest time. I didn't do any meaningful sign work for a couple of months. I just thought about Doc. Who he was and what he did and what all that slicing of the mother shark and throwing away the babies meant. A month or two before he killed himself there were ugly charges about ugly work— and a lawsuit. The city paper picked it up: "Girl dies. Doctor named in abortion case."

Authorities confiscated his records and closed his clinic. And Doc slit his own throat with one of his antique razors.

Mrs. Hensley got the country club house and the horses. Doc willed me the Lincoln. The car is tied up in tarps out back. The battery is dead by now. I found his doctor's black bag, with syringes, pituitrin and other obstetrical drugs and paraphernalia, in the trunk. I didn't feel like tooling around the valley in Doc's Lincoln. Bird shit and tree sap were ruining the finish. So I tarped it.

At the hearing Carlotta told the judge, and the *Tribune* reported all the testimony, that she had helped Doc perform many abortions. "That was his line of work" was the simple quote.

Now when I see Carlotta we talk mostly about Doc. We'll have a couple of beers and share stories about the old times. She'll come over and I'll show her some neon and how it's done. I've been trying to get someplace with my Ute Grill fish sign for weeks. Sometimes, like tonight, when we're together in bed she'll do things Doc taught her. Doc had quite a practice, as I piece it together from Carlotta's stories: Carlotta, some of the women patients, Carlotta *and* the patients. Doc the knife! Doc the shark! But his life, like mine here now in my would-be studio/bedroom—with Carlotta sleeping in the buff and curled up childlike in the reflection of my subdued but spectacular neon double-rainbow sign—had its dark colors and its light ones: separate, sequenced, starting . . . blending, and ending. The trick is to keep glowing and humming.

Carlotta wants to take a little vacation together; maybe down to the Downs at Ruidoso in memory of Doc. Lately I've been wanting to see Vegas and the grand neon masterpieces on the strip. Ideas are starting to come about the Ute Grill fish. Doc's legacy to me is not the Lincoln. It's the will to live and to see, to avoid falling into Doc's dark, bottomless pit of despair and death. There's nothing worse than total darkness to a neon sign man, a "neonate," like me. Doc used that word on the boat, I remember. I looked it up too—just as now I look much beyond my rainbow "Neon Signs" to see Vegas, to see . . . tigers burning bright in the forests of the night.

DELFINIA

We know nothing and can know nothing
but
the dance, to dance to a measure
contrapuntally,
Satyrically, the tragic foot.
—William Carlos Williams, *Paterson*

I WATCHED DELFINIA TRY TO MARCH INTO THE ROOM WITH THE others, single file, their steps cadenced and high, their arms swaying back and forth with all the flair of a school safety patrol on parade. The weekly break in regular classes called for such flamboyance of spring spirit and show.

On Wednesday, the first hour after lunch, I had lined up with these same boisterous classmates and walked down the long length of hall to Delfinia's room—Mrs. Garcia's room—at the south end of the building. Now it was Delfinia's turn to walk up the hall, north to my room—Mrs. Sandoval's. The difference was that Delfinia didn't walk like the rest of us. Her heavy black shoe was intended to help.

These recent weekly rehearsals, like the early spring that year, came fast upon us, marked by chatter and laughter, ready to burst into louder clamor, but still stifled out of unconscious gratitude for the chance to dance and the fear that with the wrong moves the trip would be canceled.

Dance was the reason for it all. I liked it as much as dodgeball or flag football, though I couldn't say so to the guys in my class, especially Henry. He liked recess and wrestling on the pounded schoolyard dirt much more than dancing with Patsy, Delfinia, Joanna, and the other "Los Padillas" charmers.

The first week of school that fall Henry almost broke the middle finger on my flag-yanking hand in a hold that bent bone and tendon the wrong way, sort of like Delfinia's foot. Lucky for me that Eddie, solemn-faced in his worn-out flannel shirt and torn overalls got Henry in a half nelson and made him repeat an improvised litany of words and grunts until he let me loose. I suffered almost as much as Henry did while Eddie dragged us both around in the dirt for a few minutes.

Eddie and Delfinia were probably my two best friends. But I tried hard not to show it. They weren't all that popular with my Anglo friends, really. And that's partly why I'm telling about some of this now. Their lives reached far into mine over the years. I take them with me still. Maybe memories of me still touch them too as they drive to work or shop for groceries, or catch an entertainment on TV—or experience some of the same racial taboos and tensions we all felt as children. How could the love I came to feel for Eddie as protector and for Delfinia, the two of us dancing together in school or escaping to the ditch, become embarrassment in front of my family and friends? Could I rid myself through the years of those early, conditioned prejudices? Might the telling help mitigate some of the hypocrisy?

Eddie was poor but strong. Delfinia was pretty but crippled. I was tall, skinny, and Okie Indian, with new school clothes each year that were outgrown by Christmas, sack lunches complete with napkins and desserts, one of the latest-model, two-toned Duncan yoyos, and no real problems—other than hair I couldn't train, arm muscles in need of developing, and a pimple here and there to pop.

I didn't know just how Delfinia's foot got crippled. I never really had the chance or the courage to ask her. "Polio" was a word always spoken to explain such things, or other things even more twisted. They had closed Tingley Beach because of polio—all the water slides and the great floating dock locked off limits. So I heard plenty about polio and knew something about it—how it felt, what it did to you—or at least I imagined that I knew about paralysis and the hysteria that surrounded the dreaded word "polio." The claustrophobic iron lungs on exhibit at the state fair frightened me most of all—choked me like my own secrets.

Delfinia's father brought her to school a couple of times. Funny thing about him was his scruffy look, his old clothes and hat, and the wagon he pulled. It was a kid's wagon, a red American Flyer or some such ironic brand. My first impression was that he pulled it as a kind of conveyance for Delfinia, but it was filled with a hodgepodge collection of lumber and wire, rags and cardboard. One trip I saw a small brown-paper grocery sack, marked with the smiling, yellow Piggly-Wiggly face, and packed with day-old bread. Mainly he delivered goat milk to Mrs. Crawford, a thin but feisty lady who lived alone in a big adobe house and told my sister that she was on a special diet "because of my stomach." Delfinia's father's official job was as a dishwasher at Dirty Fred's Cafe on the corner of Bridge and Sunset. Later Delfinia told me that it was her wagon and that her father, Firmin, had pulled her in it when she was a small girl, to help her get around.

One night I had pretended to be paralyzed in my bed while listening to a new episode of "Sergeant Preston," and that empathized specter of "polio" always rose up to meet me when I watched Delfinia walk, or when I danced with her.

Just simple walking looked painful for her, with her platform-soled shoe. She never really winced or cried out with pain. But you could tell she knew about pain. Once I caught a good glimpse of it in her eyes and in a quick grimace when she first attempted the dramatic kicks of "La Raspa." Maybe that wasn't pain I saw but human misery, Matthew Arnold's and Sophocles's eternal note of sadness. Most people with a foot like that wouldn't even try to dance. And most of the guys in her room and mine avoided dancing with her— maybe because of prejudice, or cruel streaks, or maybe because of some strange, protective kindness.

While Eddie hardly ever smiled, Delfinia always smiled. She didn't just smile, she beamed and radiated, lit up the room, all those things smiles can do and more. Her smile was its own kind of dance and it made me want to dance along. She had a complexion made all the more alive when flushed and chapped from the wind and weather since she spent a lot of time outside taking care of her mother's goats. Her mother, Lucinda, helped clean house for Mrs. Crawford, and I saw her there once, her head covered with a smooth, simple black scarf.

At recess all during the fall and winter that year Delfinia had the habit of moistening her lips with a scratched and bent black tube of ChapStick that seemed magical in its powers, and never-ending in its supply. She would even touch that tube to her chapped cheeks, especially one scarred spot that looked like a small crater, probably caused by chicken pox.

In the spring a natural moistness returned to the air and restored the softness of Delfinia's cheeks, but she refused to relinquish her winter/fall security, that old tube of ChapStick. Her teeth showed long and strong in the wide whiteness of her smile—all set against her river-brown skin, her soulful brown eyes, and long, lustrous black hair. She held her hair with a pink barrette that looked older and more precious and necessary to her than her ChapStick.

Hers was a face, a beautiful Hispanic face, that canceled out the limps and stumbles of her best-performed dance, steps that looked so painful as to bring tears to her eyes and anguish to her soft, pocked face. But would-be tears somehow surfaced in various disguises of laughter, aided by the balm of her special ChapStick.

This week's dance session was a rehearsal for the spring program, where the teachers would pass out report cards and award certificates. All the kids would dance for the crowd. Mr. Wiles, the principal, would play "Abide with Me," "The Bells of Saint Mary's," or "Moonlight Sonata" on the piano, the parents would listen and applaud, and then after some refreshments we would be sent off for the summer and, this particular year, on to new friends, feats, and defeats at high school. That's how I imagined it—continuing school with the class. But Delfinia would change things for me.

Mrs. Garcia and Mrs. Sandoval took turns explaining which dances would come where on the program, how we were to move with the rhythms of the music, and how, when we heard "Cielito Lindo" begin, we were to exit through the front doors and fall into formations under the flagpole. There would be "Cielito Lindo," "La Varsuviana," and then, for an encore, "La Raspa." I got paired with Delfinia again. I didn't mind, though I acted like I did and made the necessary frowns and grimaces for Maraga and Eddie and the others. Delfinia and I were to walk in the processional together, going and coming, and be partners in all the dances.

Maraga and Louie kidded me about it with hoots and backslaps and raised eyebrows in imitation of Groucho Marx and "You Bet Your Life." Louie even threw in a few quacks, pretended to be George Finneman and pointed to the bad-luck duck coming down on its string. Manuel flicked a *tatonie* at me. Nothing mean really. Nothing like Henry's surly stares. He threw me the symbolic *chingada* and I felt last September's injured finger's ache flare up. None of the guys wanted to be stuck with Delfinia and her deformed gait.

So the phonograph was turned on, the records were played, and we all went through our paces toward the scratchy-sounding imperfections of the day and the big spring awards program to come. Delfinia and I defiantly twisted and twirled like two animated characters out of the Sunday comic strips, as we marched through Mrs. Sandoval's door together in our own kind of mocked-up and make-believe spring program formation. When I saw the pain in her eyes and somehow gleaned a feeling not just for her sadness but for *la tristeza de la vida,* I asked her if she was okay.

"The ditch," she said. "Meet me, Gillie, by the irrigation gate. After school."

"Sure," I said under my breath, and glanced around, embarrassed, as I let go of her sticky, sweat-dampened hand and sent her off back down the hall to her room with her classmates—most of them now raucous and totally out of formation, trying to see who could jump high enough to touch the buffalos in the plains mural painted along the middle section of the corridor just outside Mr. Wiles's office.

Maraga did it first. He hit the head of the biggest beast. Maraga could do everything, and had even done "IT," he bragged, with Joanna behind the classroom annex parked out behind the baseball field. Eddie vouched for him and I never doubted Eddie. Down at Mrs. Argo's store Maraga had shown Manuel and me a tiny eight-page "Bible" ("My manual, *ese,* Manuel," he claimed), and that gave Eddie's story even more credibility. Skinny Manuel laughed and cursed and got a big kick out of that—"Jodido!" he kept saying. Just behind the baseball field and Maraga's annex ran the mother ditch, *La Acequia Madre.*

When I went back into the room Mrs. Sandoval stopped me by

her desk, motioned for me to come closer, and said in her familiar mothering voice, "That was nice of you to dance with Delfinia that way, Gilbert. You seemed to have fun and I think Delfinia did too."

"Sure," was all I could say again. "What would Mrs. Sandoval say about *La Acequia Madre?*" I thought, and I wandered to my desk and more wondering about the ditch.

Mrs. Sandoval's words coming from the front of the class never reached back to register anything. Even Eddie's over-his-shoulder glances blurred into the blackboard as I thought of my past times at the ditch. It was a special, marvelous place in the spring. Just a few weeks earlier my father had asked me, as was the seasonal cycle, to get out the shovels and help him clear the small irrigation ditch back to the big ditch, the mother ditch, *La Acequia Madre*. We cleared out debris, weeds, and trash and set fire to all such obstructions. We built up the banks and checked all the gates. The willows by the mother ditch were out, and the water was rolling along, new and muddy and red from the river, and crested with white, spumy foam, ready to be released into all the little ditches that kept the wild asparagus and the valley alfalfa fields and gardens growing through the warm summer months to come.

By now, in late April, wild asparagus was starting to poke through the ground all along the ditchways, and the birds—the meadowlarks and yellowhammers—were back, flying from the orchards to the ditches and stopping in the changing grass and bushes or in the elms and cottonwoods.

In the evening the doves stopped along the ditch for gravel and shelter, and the nighthawks beeped above the watered fields, swooping for insects, and for an hour before sunset the crows flew up the ditch on their way to roost at the river. Once at dusk I caught my breath and watched a great horned owl turn its large round head, blink, and look down at me from the giant cottonwood where the ditch ran through the culvert and under the road by Mrs. Crawford's tin-roofed, thick-walled house. I remember that the wind ruffled the owl's speckled feathers, made to look all the softer against the hard tin grayness of Mrs. Crawford's roofline, just before the big, stubby bird hooted and lurched slowly away.

In a short time I would be able to head out on an asparagus-gathering expedition and wander the smaller ditches skirting the big alfalfa field, which Mrs. Crawford hired Firmin to irrigate and mow.

The *tatonies* were out on the cottonwood trees now, and in the pockets of all us "rowdies" were clustered green and hard and waiting for a strategic throw. Manuel, the *tatonie* keeper, was the one to see when supplies got low. And more than one spring clod fight had already seen combatants lining the ditch banks, throwing and ducking those ugly exploding dirt grenades, accompanied by the yells of triumph or escape.

The ditch mothered its own special spring rituals, drawing us to her for pleasure and injury, bringing marks of manhood, real and imagined. In the summer there would be swimming in the sequestered hole just past Crawford's culvert, where the pressurized water dug into the churning sand, deep enough for us to dive in murky water much over our heads—risking collision with broken bottles, dead branches, stray baling wire, and other ditch debris.

Once Eddie and I had tried to watch as two older kids, Lannie and Yvonne, waded across the ditch in chest-deep water and then clinched on the far bank before they rolled into the willows out of sight. Eddie said that was the second time for him to see IT.

"Maraga knows more about doing IT," Eddie said, proud of his bantam *carnal*.

I wanted to know the difference between Maraga's and Lanny's techniques. One spring while ditch cleaning with my father I saw him pick up a dirt-speckled, shriveled white rubber with his shovel and, with a silent grin, toss it dangling into the ditch. Eddie's older brother, Rosendo, told us that the first thing to do was to put your arm around a girl and then squeeze—and repeat as needed. "Rosendo's recipe," Eddie called it.

I thought of that, and Delfinia's face, while I waited for the final bell to dismiss school. The ditch definitely had its enticements and adventures, and, for me, its doubts and guilts. Although a solitary and sublime place, somehow the news of ditch doings always reached back to school, back even to neighborhood, family, and home. The "dirtiness" of the ditch—its muddy, turning water, its wildness—were not endorsed by adults, at least not teachers and mothers, sisters and "nice" girls. Most frightening of all was the ditch rider. The county conservancy district sent out a ditch rider to check, repair, and report. Seldom seen and always talked about, he became a local myth. No one wanted to meet up with the ditch rider. But Delfinia had asked.

When the final bell rang, I headed out of the room toward the ditch, telling Eddie and Manuel only that I couldn't go with them down to Argo's store for the usual after-school feast—a Butternut bar, or Coke and "Tom's" brand salted peanuts. Everyone would tease me if they found out I planned to meet Delfinia there, regardless of what we did or didn't do. Like the ditch itself, Delfinia's invitation was impossible to resist. My strides increased as I passed beyond the baseball field and the annex and began my adventurous climb up the near bank of *La Acequia Madre*.

As I topped the bank, the main irrigation gate stood farther to the south and I turned and walked that way. After one bend of the ditch Delfinia came into view. She was sitting on the weathered wooden frame that supported the big steel wheel and gears of the main gate, which released the powerful stream of water into the network of smaller ditches.

She had made a reed whistle and was trying to coax out a high-pitched sound, with only some screechy success. Her cloth book satchel rested on the two-by-eight board that crossed the ditch directly over the gate itself.

She looked up and greeted me with the words "Can you make these things whistle right?"

"I can try." And I took the moist reed from her mouth, pinched it at a slightly different place, below another raised joint, and blew softly into it. The sound was not much better than hers: "Whooooo," like blowing on a pop bottle down at Argo's.

"We should join the band next year," she said with a short, swallowed laugh. "I wouldn't like the marching, though," and she looked sideways at me and broke into her enticing smile.

"Dancing is better than marching," I said.

"I think it's you that makes me like the dancing, and not the other way around. Anyway, it's fun with you."

"No kidding. Anytime."

Then Delfinia said more to me than ever before: "I was paralyzed for a long time, and when I could move, my foot was this way—not with the shoe—but, you know, this way. They said I was lucky. I feel . . . thankful to be able to move my leg, but . . . ," and she took out her old ChapStick from her blouse pocket, turned the base and touched the tube to her mouth, moved it slowly across her top lip and back across the bottom one, and then pursed them both a couple of times.

Then she took her finger and transferred some of the salve to the scar on her cheek before replacing the cap and placing the tube back into her pocket.

"You do that all the time," I said.

"Do you want to try some? Here, let me do it." And she reached into her blouse pocket again and took the tube out. "Come here . . ."

But the tube dropped in the ditch dirt and never touched my lips. What touched me were her lips, still coated with soothing, menthol-like salve. My heart churned inside my chest. I closed my eyes and heard the ditch water swish behind us as I kissed Delfinia in return. Reflexively I reached down, felt the dirt and picked up the sand-spattered ChapStick and tried to return it directly to her blouse.

Then, suddenly, grating words reached us from the distance up the ditch: "Freeze where you are, troublemakers, bastard juvenile delinquents!"

We looked up to see, through the willows, the ditch rider leaving his dusty turquoise-colored pickup, not bothering to slam the door with the black county conservancy letters bannered across it, pulling down his big-brimmed hat and attempting to move his big-bellied body and run with giant strides up the ditch bank. I could see the roll of fat hanging over his shiny, fake rodeo champion belt buckle, could see his worn and scuffed cowboy boots shooting out from the legs of his Levi's as he slipped and slid back on the clods of ditch dirt. The radio from his pickup hummed out the muffled words of Marty Robbins singing about Rose's cantina—"Down in the West Texas town of El Paso."

We had to move fast. "Across the ditch. Give me your hand," I said and pulled her up.

We turned toward the irrigation gate. In her fright Delfinia nudged past me, but she didn't step up to the two-by-eight board bridge.

"Leave the books!" and she started across the four-inch pipe next to it that braced the gate and bridged the ditch. I had walked across the long pipe before, all twenty feet of it, and it took great nimble-footed talent. For Delfinia it would be impossible. But in that excited, frightened moment we were on the pipe before I comprehended the reality of the challenge before us. Delfinia stepped out with her left foot and then slid her heavy-shoed right foot up to meet it. Behind that came my hand holding tight, and my own goat-footed balancing act. Delfinia led, created her own step, and I followed, trying to duplicate the step-slide-wobble she had devised and now settled into a pattern.

Somehow fear turned to urgent fun. We concentrated. We forgot. We remembered. We moved to the rhythms of our own invention and we glided over the smooth pipe while the waters of the ditch flowed under us, before us, behind us, around us.

The threatening, taunting sounds of the ditch rider and the dark shadow of Delfinia's shoe faded into a creamy-white blanket of ditch foam floating on the surface of the water, and then we were on the other side. We had crossed over the water, danced over and across it. And once across we were still dancing the ditch.

The ditch rider had made it up the rolling clods and was trotting down the ditch bank, to the words and music of "El Paso," as fast as he could manage it. I grabbed Delfinia's arm and jerked her after me as we started to run down the ditch levee toward our own kind of border freedom: the culvert and the main road by Mrs. Crawford's house. There we clopped down the ditch bank and hid behind the giant cottonwood, gasping and trying to be quiet, trying to hold our frightened laughter.

We heard the ditch rider stop at the culvert to wait for a car to whip by. With his big gut to carry he was too winded to continue the chase, so he yelled out his staccato curse: "Damn you destructive bastards! Stay away from my gates! I'll report you to old Wiles."

We leaned our heads back against the rough trunk of the tree and looked up into the mixture of brown and green and blue. I watched the clusters of *tatonies* move with the breeze. I reached into my Levi's pocket and retrieved the ChapStick.

"You forgot this back there," I said and handed it to Delfinia.

She took off the cap and put the pleasant-smelling balm to her lips, sighed long and hard, looked at me and laughed warmly, knowingly, through her smile, and threw the tube into the flowing waters of the ditch.

"Let's see if you can fold this cottonwood leaf into a whistle, Gilbert."

What happened next was the jubilant, spontaneous culmination of our partnership. There in the willows and sand the ditch and spring overtook us completely in new rhythms of excitement. We swooned together in the spring surges of the mother ditch's encompassing embrace.

We rid ourselves of all fear and guilt, the stigma of the ditch. Delfinia's strange shoes rested beside us, and my eyes moved to her foot expecting the worst of deformities . . . only to see that it was just smaller and that her right leg was stunted but perfectly formed, just smaller than normal.

"It's not ugly, is it, Gillie? Just different," she said as she moved to the bank of the ditch and sat with her feet in the moving water so that her legs looked of perfectly equal length.

"No, not ugly," I replied as I sat down by her side, and dangled my bare feet in the ditch water too. Together we watched the spindly, long-legged water spiders skim and dance over the surface of the brown, slowing backswirls.

I realized how outrageous my fears had been, how horrible I had expected her foot to look. But even that fear, such as it was, transformed itself into happiness—for now we knew, and shared, the hitherto hidden secret of Delfinia's deformed beauty.

From inside the front doors I could see the flags flapping hard in the wind at the top of the tall flagpole planted in the sprawling cement circle in front of the school. Beneath the red, white, and blue of the Stars and Stripes, the yellow-and-red Zia sun State of New Mexico flag popped and cracked from the high wind currents bouncing over the school roofline and colliding with the crudely crafted, oversized letters of our "Los Padillas" identity.

Mr. Finley, the janitor, strained at the long horizontal metal bars to keep the giant doors open wide enough so we could hear "Cielito Lindo" when Mrs. Sandoval decided to tell Manuel to "start his engine," turn up the volume and adjust the tone of the big bell-shaped loudspeaker.

The rehearsed idea was for Mrs. Sandoval to signal Mrs. Garcia (stationed across the doorway from Mr. Finley), who would then squeeze Maraga's neck and send us marching through the doors to perform. I could see Mrs. Sandoval looming over the awards table and giving directions to Manuel, who, serving as her *mayordomo,* arranged the phonograph records, turned all the appropriate knobs, and kept parents and visitors from tripping on the extension cords, disturbing the stack of report cards, or knocking over the award case with all the certificates.

Mr. Rushing was just finishing directing the six or seven kids who tried to play violins and plastic flutes for him for an hour each morning. Their last number was "Long, Long Ago," but, like "Old Black Joe" before it, all you could hear was the chain, keeping its own mischievous tempo, banging against the flagpole.

"Get ready, all you jackrabbits," yelled Mrs. Garcia as she started to walk back down the line to shake everybody back in place.

Henry was hunkering in a corner with a couple of his buddies while their dance partners tittered away. Eddie was standing strong and silent next to tiny Virginia Mora, who was hiding her face behind her hands and looked ready for a heart attack. His Thom McCann shoes had a fresh treatment of Esquire Scuff-Coat and he wore a brand-new flannel shirt from El Cambio supermarket. Maraga and Joanna had their arms around each other, and Delfinia and I, next in line, held hands behind them. I snapped the top pearl snap of my dress-only, maroon-and-gold cowboy shirt and rubbed the toes of my tan cowboy boots on the back pant legs of my stiff new Levi's.

The strains of "Cielito Lindo" started: "Ay, ay, ay, ay . . . ," and Mr. Finley opened the doors wide and dropped the doorstops with a bang, Mrs. Garcia grabbed Maraga by the back of the neck and shoved, and we were on our way, keeping step to the counter-point of the flagpole chain and the softer sounds of the phonograph's scratchy voicings and the words "Come a-long—where there's dance and song, / For we love you, Cie-li-to Lin-do. . . ."

Delfinia was loved and lovely in her homemade, silver-hemmed, turquoise fiesta skirt and her light-blue anklets with ruffled tops turned down over the ankle of her left shoe and the high top of her platformed right one. She wore a red sash around her waist and some little wild roses in her hair, held with her pink barrette and a couple of extra bobby pins.

We walked surely and cautiously down the endless concrete steps and then marched more rapidly around the flagpole and then beyond it, onto the wide concrete slab, trying all the while to buck the wind, which caused Delfinia and Virginia and the rest of the girls some embarrassment, since they were supposed to hold their partners' hands and still keep the gusts of wind from lifting their dresses. Joanna seemed not to care about the wind and its designs on her dress and the ribbons in her hair.

Mr. Wiles stood next to the awards table and beside the school upright piano that had been rolled outside for the occasion. He was rubbing his hands and waiting for the big finale of his piano solos, which would end the program. Across from him, lining the other side of our improvised concrete stage floor, teachers and parents and other relatives sat talking and gawking in row after row of Mr. Finley's folding chairs.

After the turns around the pole and a circle or two of our concrete dance floor, we pulled up short and took our group positions for the next song. Manuel removed the phonograph needle from "Cielito Lindo" with a distorted, screechy zip, put on another record, and started up the sweet fiddle sounds of the introduction to the main melody of the song. I put my arm around Delfinia and held her right hand tightly, while she reached her left hand up to join mine next to my chest. Then the cue words, faster than usual: "Put your little foot, put your little foot, put your little foot right here," and almost together we all began the dance.

Delfinia looked at me and smiled as we finished the first set of steps pretty much with the other dancers. Manuel had the record

speed set at 78 rpm rather than 45. Even at normal rehearsal speed
Delfinia had to slide her small foot and overbuilt shoe part of the way
rather than just lift it up and point it daintily in front of her. This faster
speed made it harder, but also funnier. My sharp-toed cowboy boot
made a bizarre contrast to Delfinia's big, blunt shoe. Her shoe. My
boot. We didn't exactly have a "little foot" to put "right here"—or
anywhere. All my rehearsing over the past weeks had been done in
my regular school shoes. Now I had a hard time keeping my balance
because of the narrow, canted heels on my boots, and trying to adjust
to Delfinia's delayed step made things worse. I knew we were thinking the same thing—dancing the ditch! We were doing a slide, step,
wobble similar to the one that we did when we walked the irrigation
gate pipe to escape the ditch rider that special, short time ago.

"Lin-do, Lin-do, Lin-do," came the repeated words of the now-
stuck record.

Mrs. Sandoval could be heard issuing loud commands to her
mayordomo:"Manuel, it's stuck at the wrong speed. For heaven's
sake fix that, . . . fix that!" echoed her well-grooved words.

Mr. Wiles was wringing rather than warming his hands, now
positioned in front of his quivering chin. Maraga and Joanna were
breaking into some twirls that looked much more like a clumsy *rio
arriba* polka hop crossed with a cool jitterbug step. Eddie and
Virginia stopped dead in their tracks, giggling. Even Henry and
Florinda changed their scowls and frowns into broad grins as they
kept trying to follow the instructions of the rapid-fire lyrics.

The flagpole chain clanged louder and dresses flared higher as
the wind gusted stronger and picked up sand and dust—and a pile of
tumbleweeds waiting by the side school wall. Then the sand hit hard
into our faces and someone screamed, *"Mucho ojo!* Here come the
tumbleweeds!"

They tumbled and jumped over tables and chairs, swirled up and
dove down, sucked up the report cards, knocked open the award-
certificate case, and spun and twisted in their own frantic dance,
streaking and splattering toward the concrete slab as if it were a giant
target, a bull's-eye and not an improvised dance floor. Adults,
teachers, kids—everyone was ducking for cover, running out of the

way of the brittle, dry, dancing dervishes and their accompanying flying wads of paper and pellets of sand, dirt, and tiny rocks.

Delfinia and I first knelt down on the concrete together and tried to cover our heads. She used her sweater. I cradled my eyes and nose in the crook of one arm, while I tried to deflect the malevolent, thorny tumbleweeds. Then we ran fast—this time for the shelter of the school building with the others, but our thoughts were of our ditch dance.

"Remember the Alamo, *hermanos!*" shrieked Maraga.

"I've got Louie's report card. You passed! You passed!" someone shouted over the whir of the wind.

"I want my award certificate," whined Patsy as she took off toward the street, chasing the swirling papers.

Mr. Finley was at the doors like a khaki-clad Saint Peter at the gates of heaven. Two guardian angels, Mrs. Sandoval and Mrs. Garcia, were shepherding the stray kids: "Hurry, hurry, kids. Duck for cover," they repeated as the welcome trio gathered us in.

Delfinia and I turned back to look at the storm. The tumbleweeds were still bouncing along in the wind, over the baseball field, past Maraga's annex, dancing toward . . . the ditch. One after the other they hit the thick willows along the bank and lodged there, some on top of the others, bunching and thrusting and clustering—trying to escape, to cross the ditch like we had, but subdued by the green willows and the coursing waters of the mother ditch.

Delfinia, trying to wipe some of the sand out of the corners of her eyes, blinked rapidly and asked, "Any dirt in my eyes?" They were red and tearing.

"No dirt. Just your eyes."

"We didn't finish our dance. We didn't get our dancing awards. School is over now and we won't be here, dancing, again."

I felt the gritty residue of the sandstorm in my eyes—and my throat. I had secretly planned to see Delfinia forever, had wanted to walk the small ditches together in a perpetual present, gathering spring asparagus and wild dill while watching the meadowlarks and doves. I longed to dance the mother ditch with her again. I saw us releasing the flowing, loving irrigation waters of *La Acequia Madre* into the hot, purple-flowered alfalfa fields of summer. But what would my parents, my sister, my buddies say?

Today was supposed to celebrate the beginnings of spring, mark our commencement together, Anglo/Indio, and Hispanic into a careless summer. But school was over and that would no longer "classify" us as classmates, no longer salve our socially sanctioned "public" friendship. Class differences of another kind would release us into separate waterways of life.

We both knew it. I unsnapped my shirt flap and reached two fingers down into my pocket to find the gift. I looked at the new black tube of ChapStick, warm from my body and my heart's syncopated beat.

"Our dancing award?" I asked as I held it out to her—and though I didn't fully realize it then in quite the same way, to the ditch rider, to Mr. Wiles and Mr. Finley, to Mrs. Garcia and Mrs. Sandoval, to Henry and Eddie, Louie and Joanna and Maraga, to the dance, to . . . "Satyrically, the tragic foot." To Delfinia and the mother ditch.

VALEDICTION

Our two soules therefore, which are one,
Though I must goe, endure not yet
A breach, but an expansion,
Like gold to ayery thinnesse beate.
—John Donne, "A Valediction: Forbidding Mourning"

DRESSED IN HIS SHINY-SEATED PENNEY'S SUIT AND SMELLING OF
Aqua Velva and May morning air, he drove up Rio Grande Boulevard
at a good clip. He had five minutes to make it to the intersection at
Candelaria Road. His tradition. He owed it to the routine and ritual of
his second year of traveling the same route to make it today. Routine.
On time. Again.

If Friday morning traffic held at the same flow, his usual
swooping right turn would place him at the traffic light at 7:45. A
heavy punch to the accelerator with his thick-soled brogues, then a
jerk into high gear—a resolution into a cruising speed of 55 miles per
hour up Candelaria—and he would make it, would pull up in the
parking lot at 7:56. He would be at his classroom door by 8:00. On
time. Ready to convene his homeroom, make the necessary end-of-
the-year announcements to his sophomores, and shepherd them
across the quad to the gym for the ceremonies at 8:30.

The band would play the school song. The drill squad and
cheerleaders would do their maroon-and-gold glittery thing. The
coaches would give out their respective athletic letters. The jocks
would thank all the loyal Viking "supporters"—proud of their win-
loss record and their word play. Old man Dixon would announce
honor society membership and pass out the usual mix of music and
club certificates of achievement. And he would carry out his assem-

bly assignment: patrol the rest rooms one last time. Graduation ceremonies would be Sunday afternoon. Then, until next fall, it was good-bye, Valley High!

A couple of weeks off and then he would have to hit the books himself. Six more semester credits and he would be at the next salary level and ready to take his M.A. examinations. Then a teaching load of college prep juniors and advanced placement seniors and a gross of eight thousand dollars a year! No more of this "remedial reading," which had taken so much of his energy; trying to teach these know-it-alls how to read the simplest English had just about sapped all his twenty-two-year-old's stamina. This final day of school was long in coming. His mind drifted back and forth between his classroom "challenge," his troubles during the year with Demetrio and the course in seventeenth-century English poetry: Lovelace and Marvell, and Donne. Herbert, Vaughan, Crashaw, and George Crabbe. "Carpe diem." Wit and conceits and the Metaphysicals. . . . Donne and Demetrio! Now there was a farfetched "yoking of opposites," as Dr. Johnson would say.

His "man-made-materials" briefcase rested at the ready next to him in the front seat of the '53 Chevy which served him loyally (through sun and flash floods, dust storms and tumbleweeds) as a work car—his only car. The radio's volume knob was broken but movable. The dash was chipped and the glove compartment stayed ajar. The right rear door was caved in, the original strip of chrome molding was missing from fender to fender, and only one dented hubcap decorated the passenger side of the jalopy. Only the letters *g l i d* remained of the original "Powerglide" molded lettering, and they hung free, suspended by one small metal brad. The motor needed a valve job. The transmission bands were shot.

The purchase price of the car had been a hundred bucks at Abe Gibson's Discount Autos. Autumn before last, when Gibson heard him say, "my first year teaching at Valley High," he made a special deal: "Well, what do you say. All my kids go there. I'll knock off fifty and sell it to you at a steal—$98.99. And I'll even throw in an extra six quarts of oil!"

Sure enough, he finally did have one of Gibson's kids in his class this year, in the last-hour remedial reading class—Martha, with the smiling face and the stuttering speech that marked her as the slowest reader in the whole class. At least now she spoke up and could be heard.

Not like Demetrio and his habitual mumble. His grimacing. His letter-by-letter finger pointing. Those first weeks had been sheer anger. Breaking of pencils. Pounding of desks. Gestures and acts of belligerence against classmates. Then sullen defiance. Then he miraculously took his turn and tried to read out loud with the class. Into February and he was actually participating. Even raising his hand and offering to comment. By April he tried to write a book report. Then a final class theme on *A Green Light for Sandy.* Martha's final composition of the year was in his briefcase with the others—with Rosendo's and Nora's and the rest. With Demetrio's.

He saw the Candelaria green light ahead and checked the mirror to move to the turning lane, he pushed up the turn-signal lever, and reached over with his right hand to steady the briefcase, rubbing the flaking gold-embossed initials "MJ" briefly with his thumb as he grasped the steering knob with his left hand and began the familiar swooping turn that had marked the start of so many days for him that year—and the year before.

It was a turn he enjoyed. For sure. And as he released the knob and let the free-spinning steering wheel straighten out the old Chevy, he tromped the gas pedal with a "bombs away" feeling as the fresh air hit his face, causing the tissue paper he had used to stanch a shaving wound to flutter in the wind like a World War I aviator's scarf.

When the transmission finally caught and the speedometer needle climbed to 55 miles per hour cruising speed, he reached up and pulled off the thin, bloodstained paper and offered it as morning sacrifice to the winds of spring. To green lights everywhere and for all! His toast. Especially for Demetrio and the others whose words he had spent a year listening to and reading, pronouncing and correcting; for all those whose book reports, whose writings, he now transported.

It had been a crisp morning like this when he first became Demetrio's teacher. When Mr. Dixon told him that the last scheduled class of his day would be "remedial reading" and would pool "slow learners" and "discipline problems" from all the language arts classes and give them to an energetic, ambitious young teacher, to him.

"No use arguing, now," he remembered Dixon saying. "It's a needed class. You have extra course work in English, and . . . you're the last one hired. Think of it as the luck of the draw, my boy. Only ten kids. That's the good thing about it. Consider it a challenge."

No mind that the extra course work was one summer, last summer, studying American literary realism and naturalism. No matter that when he glanced at the class list and saw Demetrio's name he knew he had trouble. He had personally marched the boy to Dixon's office for smoking in the rest rooms and for calling him a *Cabron*, to his face. In retaliation Demetrio and other *compadre vatos*, his buddies, had greeted him next morning—a human barricade. And all of them smoking!

He glanced quickly at his briefcase, remembering that he had placed it in front of him and pushed through the wall of bodies and smoke and taunts of "trucha," and "cuidado," and nonchalantly unlocked his classroom door—afraid and furious and pretending to ignore them.

That tense time stayed in his mind as he looked at his watch, let up on the accelerator, pulled down the turn-signal lever, lightly braked, and turned left into the school parking lot. It was 7:59.

He noticed the crowd of students lined up on the sidewalk, some of them sitting on the curb, some of them in front of the effusive, yellow-flowering forsythia. They held a banner. There was a small band—a couple of trumpets, a sax and clarinet, a drum! Rosendo held a small accordion! He could hear the strains of the school song. Demetrio was in front—with Martha, smiling her widest, brightest smile and looking like a Valley High version of Botticelli's *Primavera*. Nora, Louis, Sammy, Rosendo, Duane, Irving, Larry . . . they were all there. They were waving.

He looked over the steering wheel and under the rickety sun visor, looked intently through the windshield and read the banner, in alternating maroon and yellow: "Thanks, M.J." He pulled to a stop and set the emergency brake. He grabbed his briefcase and, amid the music and the voices, got out of the car.

"Hey! What's this?" he tried to yell over the noise. "I know . . . you're all wanting *A*'s, right? Payola's out of the question. I can't be bribed."

It wasn't out of the question. Not the way he felt at that moment. He could be. "I've already graded your reports. They're in my briefcase, ready to turn back to you." He could feel the sun on his neck and face, the slight burn and itch of the razor wound fast healing on his face. He was blushing!

The band dwindled to a silence, and Martha stepped to the front of the group and said, "Mmister Jjhons. Ddemetrio has ssomething tto read, a sspeech and a ggood-bye ggift."

He smiled and stood there in the spring-bright sun, in joyous disbelief, holding his briefcase with both hands and at arm's length down in front of him, a courier captive to his valise.

"Martha, . . . you've got to be kidding about all this. Are you guys for real? Serious?" They all yelled in unison, "Yes. Yes." And someone squawked a few rally notes on the sax. Rosendo echoed it with a run on his squawk box. Mister Johns saw some sparrows in the forsythia.

Demetrio replaced Martha in front of the group. He held a small wooden object under one arm, and in his hand was a piece of yellow theme paper. He wore starched, creased khakis. His black, sharp-pointed shoes glistened and shined and reflected the sunny brightness of the musical instruments. His shirt was buttoned securely at the neck, and the long shirttail reached over his pants pockets. His black hair flowed from a full wave over his forehead back into a neatly tapered ducktail. Mr. Johns noticed the crudely tattooed cross between thumb and forefinger on the hand that held the paper. Then Demetrio began to read:

> Dear Mr. Johns. Thanks you for helping us read and
> write. We are happy that you were our teacher. We are
> happy that we ended the year with you. We liked the book
> about Sandy's success. We want that too. We are sorry for
> trouble. Have a good summer. Your students. P.S. I done
> this for you in shop. Goodbye. Demetrio Tafoya

Demetrio handed him the yellow piece of notepaper and took the wooden object from under his arm and handed it to him. It was a book stand, crafted out of mahogany, sanded smooth with pumice and covered with several coats of varnish and rubbed linseed oil. He took the book stand and shook Demetrio's hand. Martha laughed and began clapping. And the makeshift band started the strains of the school fight song again.

He opened his briefcase and handed out the themes. He hoped his summer papers on John Donne fared as well. At the top of each paper was a bold and proud *A* circled in green.